LOADER

LOADER

SETI Man

Dudley Price

Matador
Unit E2 Airfield Business Park,
Harrison Road, Market Harborough,
Leicestershire. LE16 7UL
Tel: 0116 2792299
Email: books@troubador.co.uk
Web: www.troubador.co.uk/matador
Twitter: @matadorbooks

ISBN 978 1805140 269

British Library Cataloguing in Publication Data.
A catalogue record for this book is available from the British Library.

Printed and bound by CPI Group (UK) Ltd, Croydon, CR0 4YY
Typeset in 11pt Minion Pro by Troubador Publishing Ltd, Leicester, UK

Matador is an imprint of Troubador Publishing Ltd

This story is for
Susan Avis

To the moon and back

Absence of evidence
is not
evidence of absence

Carl Sagan,
astronomer, 1934–1996

PROLOGUE

MOSCOW. JANUARY.

Alex Andropov stared unseeingly from the window of his second-floor office onto Lubyanka Square. It was late afternoon, the light failing early. A cold wind drove biting snow across the enormous square; at its far side, figures hurried along the pavement, shoulders bowed into the snow and heads huddled into their collars, making their way to car parks and buses.

Behind Andropov was his large office, a high-ceiled room; it was part of the complex that had been home to the notorious KGB, long since removed from the building and reformed elsewhere as the FSB.

A small suite of offices remained, secretive, without name plaques.

The room's sparse furnishing comprised a large, old-fashioned desk, Andropov's large swivel chair, two guest chairs and two filing cabinets. A lot of floor space remained, mostly polished parquet and two large carpets.

The walls, adorned with old-fashioned gilded frame pictures, lent the room a faded glamour.

On one of the guest chairs sat Dimitri Petrov, wearing

the uniform of a colonel of the army; he sat silent, impassive, waiting.

Eventually, Andropov turned and returned to the desk, subsiding heavily into his chair. The desk bore only a telephone and a single thick file; across its cover, a file number was printed centrally and in bold red letters: секретно. Top secret.

Andropov sighed, resting his hand on the file. Eventually he stirred, picking up the telephone.

The call was picked up immediately, silently.

"Get me Brown Bear." Andropov's voice was gravelly from a lifetime of smoking cheap tobacco. He waited, imagining he could hear the connections being made, first into the data room where first-level encryption was applied, then a second imagined click as the encrypted line was doubly secured, finally through the packet-switching software. Conversations or data would be transmitted in separate split-second bursts of energy. Totally secure.

Barely a minute passed before the call was answered by a cultured English voice.

"Max Turner."

Andropov's voice was gravelly, measured. "Brown Bear SIG 282230 is activated with immediate effect. Data file follows."

He pressed a red key on the telephone base unit and replaced the receiver.

The whole thick file on his desk, in digitised format, held on the mother computer, was downloaded in seconds.

Andropov picked up the paper file and handed it across the desk to Colonel Petrov.

"It's running," he said. "You can prepare phase two."

The colonel nodded, stood, tucking the file under his arm, gave a gentle click of his heel and left the room.

In a large manor house somewhere in England, its library transformed into a nerve centre, a computer beeped discreetly.

One line of text lit up.

'Brown Bear SIG482230 downloaded'.

NORTH SEA N58.3 E2.10. JANUARY. 6AM

The UK Carrier Strike Group was heading NNE at speed. The group, known as the CSG, comprised the aircraft carrier HMS *Queen Elizabeth*, flanked by two destroyers, HMS *Diamond* and HMS *Defender*. Close behind was the frigate HMS *Kent* and an RFA tanker. The CSG was scheduled to join up with the US and French Navies in a joint exercise off the Norwegian Sea.

On the bridge of the *Queen Elizabeth*, Captain Daniel Knight breathed deeply. He had felt the adrenaline running through his veins ever since they left Southampton Water; now, as he watched the escort's wakes creaming out behind, he felt exhilaration and pride that the UK Carrier Strike Group was a formidable force on par with the US and Allied Navies. He felt the responsibility for over two thousand crew members of the vessels of the combined group but also a nagging fear that the carrier was vulnerable to attack or mishap. He sometimes felt that the vast carrier, despite its awesome power, was a sitting duck, relying totally on the effectiveness of the escorting vessels.

Although the group was on a peacetime exercise, he checked yet again that all stations were operating to strict protocols.

He listened to the operations comms patched through to his position. There was a background of comms chatter as the teams went about their roles in muted voices, calmly relaying status and instructions throughout the fleet.

Then directly, a clear statement from the comms centre.

"Russian Bears incoming, sir. One hundred miles, heading west-northwest."

Knight was not surprised. But nevertheless, he felt a surge of anxiety.

"Warn them off, number one," Knight said, listening in to the transmission.

"Hello TU-90. This is Carrier Group 09240 heading north-northeast. Notified Exercise 2056 – 'Fresh Start'. You are approaching UK waters. Please stand off. Do you read?"

A reply came back immediately, in English, with only a slight accent.

"TU-90 heading on routine patrol. We have no intention to join your party. Good hunting."

"Understood, TU-90. Good day to you too. CG 2401 logged at six-thirty GMT."

Daniel Knight sighed with relief; this was a standard encounter but always left him uneasy. What if the encounter had ratcheted up?

Captain Knight patched the ops screen onto his bridge monitor and continued to watch the blip of the Russian plane as it continued its inwards move towards the fleet. He listened to routine operations chatter, the quiet voices comforting in Knight's ears.

Then a firm voice cut in from the comms station, harsh in the subdued chatter.

"We're on it, sir. Escorts scrambled and on way."

A red line had been crossed, triggering an immediate fast reaction response.

The radar blip continued its slow inwards move. Four faster blips appeared on the periphery of the monitor moving towards the incoming Russian bomber. Only when the blips appeared to merge did the incoming aircraft begin a noticeable turn not far from the twelve-mile territorial boundary.

Captain Knight gave a sigh of relief – a textbook chorography.

The Carrier Strike Group continued its course into the Norwegian Sea to meet its allies. Six capital ships of the British Navy, at pace, wakes creaming out behind them, armed, formidable.

CHAPTER 1

Matt Loader spread yesterday's national *Daily Telegraph* on the kitchen table, turning to page four. He had read the quarter page article yesterday but read it again with some satisfaction. Well, he had written it!

A thumbnail head-and-shoulder photo – showing a clean-shaven face, dark hair, greying at the temples – adorned the upper left of the article and beneath it his identity, Matthew Loader, Defence and Security Correspondent.

The text covered the story of an ongoing NATO exercise testing the formation of a strike force in which the British were taking the lead role. Loader had secured a press release photograph showing the flotilla of ships escorting the new aircraft carrier *Queen Elizabeth* steaming at speed off the north-east coast.

His reverie was cut short by the telephone ringing. He turned and lifted the receiver from the wall mount.

"Matt Loader."

A female voice responded. "Hi, Matt, this is Jan."

Janet was the PA to John Fairmount, Chief Editor of the *Daily Telegraph* newspaper.

"This is a coincidence," Matt said, "I was just looking at yesterday's piece again as you called."

"There have been a few comments already."

"All good, of course!" he quipped.

"Mainly yes. There are always a few whose aim seems to be searching for articles like yours and firing off a stream of invective. However, there was one call I think you could follow up."

"Oh, yes?"

"Well, he sounded OK, educated and that, but very serious and adamant that he should contact you."

"What about?"

"He wouldn't say but said it was of vital importance."

"What's his name?"

"Again, he wouldn't say, just wanted to meet you and that time was of the essence."

"Sounds like another oddball to me, Jan."

"OK. But he has called twice so far. He says he is a regular reader of your articles, and he could tell you things that would create a major story."

"Oh yes! Heard it all before, Jan." He paused. "I tell you what. I am coming into the office tomorrow, anyway. If he is there at about ten o'clock, I will see him."

"Righto then, I'll pass the message on. Oh, and Matt! Look forward to seeing you." There was a hint of flirtation in her voice.

Next day was bright but cold; Matt decided to walk from his Chelsea apartment to the offices in Buckingham Palace Road. He strode along the embankment as far as the bridge before joining Ebury Road then on to Buckingham Palace

Road. His walking style, gained from years in the military, ate up the distance.

Since 2006, the *Daily Telegraph* offices had been part of the Victoria Plaza development. He turned through the front arches into the glass-fronted offices. It was exactly 10am as he showed his pass to one of the staff at reception.

"Hi, Mr Loader, in today?"

"Not really, Gail, just a quick visit to check on something. Oh, and Jan said there will be a visitor for me about now – please let me know when he arrives."

Gail grinned. "He's been here an hour already." She nodded across the reception hall. "That's the gentleman in the corner. Brown coat."

"Did he give his name?"

Gail studied the visitor's screen. "Yes, George Newby, arrived ten past nine."

Loader laughed. "I'd better see him then. Thanks, Gail, see you."

He walked across the room to where the visitor was seated, away from the through traffic in the reception area.

Newby had been watching the desk and, recognising Loader, scrambled to his feet. He was fairly well built, about sixty years old with combed-back grey hair.

Loader's first impression reminded him of Ronnie Barker of the TV sitcom *Open All Hours*, even down to the long, brown coat.

After greeting, they sat facing each other. Loader got straight to the point.

"I hear that you've got a story that may be of interest to me."

Newby said, "Yes indeed, thank you for agreeing to meet me." He paused as if gathering his thoughts. "I follow your articles and I believe I have something that is right in your sphere and which you could take forward." He paused.

"OK," said Loader patiently. "What *is* the story?"

"It's big."

"And?"

Newby hesitated again, seemingly to try and frame his words.

"Well, the difficulty is that I need £600,000 for the story."

Loader laughed. "That's not the way it works here, er, George. You tell me what it's about, then maybe I can tell you what it's worth."

There was thirty seconds of silence – Newby seemed to be weighing his thoughts – then, "I've got to have £600,000."

"It can't be done, George." Loader's voice was friendly. "You've got to tell me what it's all about and then we can discuss it. If it's something that would interest our readers, or would be newsworthy, then we can discuss what it's worth."

Newby's voice became anxious. "Mr Loader, er, Matt, I don't want you to dismiss the story out of hand."

"No, OK."

There was a long pause; Newby took a deep breath. He looked at Loader.

"I'm in touch with aliens!"

Loader's heart sank. He laughed, irritably. "You're joking!" He stood up. "I think we're done here."

"*Wait*! Look, I know how it seems, but hear me out, Matt, *please*! I am not the whacko you might think. I've a PhD in astrophysics, one-time professor at the University of Birmingham; you can check my credentials."

Something in Newby's voice caused Loader to pause. "Go on."

Newby gave an audible sigh of relief.

"I've spent over twenty years on this project, Matt. I've got to where I am, but I'm stuck. I'm out of money; my wife works to keep us afloat. I just need about £600,000 to move forward."

"What project? Who's backing you?"

"Nobody's backing me. This is a personal thing. I want to keep hold of it until I am ready to announce it to the world. You could be that conduit."

"Frankly, George, it's all too far-fetched! If there is anything in what you say, the big institutions would have discovered it by now."

"Well, they haven't. Look, I'm a member of the SETI Institute; I study both the NASA releases and the Breakthrough Listen project outputs, and I am well ahead of them."

Loader stared hard at Newby.

"So, what have you got?"

"I receive intelligent signals from space and reply to them. We have a two-way contact."

Loader laughed. "You're being scammed, George. Come on!" He was again losing interest in the conversation.

"Look, Matt, I've spent a million on the research; I'm broke. Our home is mortgaged to the hilt; my wife is at her wit's end. I must get the money to complete the job. All I ask is that you come and see for yourself, but I need £600,000 for the story."

Loader was silent for a long time. Newby was clearly an educated man; he was in the middle of some sort of delusional project, but could there be a story there? He played the angles in his mind. There could be something that would amuse the reading public.

"So, what have you got, George?"

Newby fidgeted. "Not here, Matt," he said, looking around as if the reception area was filled with eavesdroppers.

"So, you've nothing to show me?"

Newby leaned in, speaking earnestly. "Oh, yes I have, Matt, but it's complex; there's a mountain of records; a lot of the evidence is digital. You need to visit us and spend a day or two."

Loader felt uneasy. There had to be a scam somewhere. Government-backed institutions spent billions probing the skies twenty-four seven. What could this loner have that merited attention?

Newby waited.

Finally, Loader decided to follow the lead a bit more.

"OK. If you can convince me that what you say is credible, and there is a story there, I am sure it would sell for £600,000 and probably much more. But, George, I won't take kindly to having my time wasted."

The tension drained from Newby's face. "Thank you, Matt," he said earnestly. "Thank you. That's all I ask. Just visit us and I can show you all the evidence you need."

"Us?"

"My wife Susan and I live in Norfolk. We have a farmhouse there."

CHAPTER 2

The UK Government has a Crisis Management Committee.

It meets in one of the Cabinet Office Briefing Rooms in Whitehall; it has become known by the acronym COBRA. (Cabinet Office Briefing Room 'A').

This day, there was a COBRA meeting called for 9am. It was in meeting room 'F'.

At 8.50am, the chancellor, Keith Brennan, and the defence secretary, Malcolm Bishop, were present; both were habitual early arrivals, the chancellor in particular, touchy about latecomers.

By 8.55am, Margaret Dibden arrived. As Head of Research, GCHQ, based in Cheltenham, she had the furthest to travel. She had left home at 5.30am.

By 9am on the dot, the chief of the defence staff, Sir Mark Forsyth entered, closely followed by Frank Gaynor, MI6 and Nigel Phillips, MI5.

Greetings were being exchanged as the foreign secretary John Toogood arrived.

"What's the amazing Grace got for us today?" he quipped to the assembly.

There was a smattering of laughs. Grace was the Right Honourable Grace Armstrong MP, Prime Minister.

Grace Armstrong was often called the Accidental Prime Minister.

A strikingly attractive woman at fifty-four, she had never sought ambition in the political world. Graduating in the field of microbiology and happier studying microscopic organisms. Her analytical mind and decisive nature took her to the top of her profession, gaining two PhDs on the way.

A national emergency involving a poisoning incident took her into centre stage of the political arena; she was persuaded to stand for parliament in her constituency and another meteoric rise followed, taking her to the top role as Prime Minister.

Now she firmly managed the affairs of the nation, controlling the Cabinet with surgical precision. Most members were happy with her style, some of whom literally swooned in her presence.

But she had some detractors, mostly those with a 'Boys' Club' mentality, who were only too aware of the disparity of qualifications between her and most ministers. Also, they were reluctant to accept orders from a female boss.

Grace Armstrong had a disarming smile, firm voice, but colleagues were wary; she took no prisoners.

Cabinet room 'F' was a large room, with high windows. Behind the head of the table, a bank of monitors adorned the wall; on one side stood a lectern and laptop.

The seven officials had availed themselves with coffee

from a side table and began to settle around the large table, leaving the top chair vacant.

They all fiddled with folders taken from their briefcases, studied mobile phones and engaged in small talk.

At 9.10am, the PA to the prime minister entered the room.

"Ladies and gentlemen, the prime minister." The aide's firm voice cut short the small talk as Grace Armstrong entered the room to stand behind the top chair.

There was a scrambling to feet with a chorus of greeting. "Prime Minister."

The defence secretary had remained seated.

The PM, hands resting lightly on the back of her chair, smiled briefly, waited impassively. The defence secretary sheepishly got to his feet.

"Good morning, everyone. Please be seated."

With a general shuffling, everyone took their seats.

Three people entered the room and took seats at the back of the room. One of whom stepped forward and placed a file in front of the seated PM. A Cabinet secretary sat at a side desk.

Grace Armstrong gazed briefly at the assembled group.

"Gentlemen, Margaret," she said, inclining her head towards the HoR, GCHQ, her voice calm, engaging.

"I believe we have a situation. Two days ago, GCHQ intercepted an encrypted signal, clearly from Russia, which seems to have activated a covert operation : Brown Bear."

Several of the COBRA members looked puzzled. "Brown Bear?"

The prime minister nodded. "Yes, it was unknown to me too until Nigel alerted me." She turned to Margaret Dibden.

"Margaret, please update us on the GCHQ findings."

Margaret Dibden picked up her file.

"Thank you, Prime Minister. Last Saturday, the same day of the last Russian incursion towards UK airspace, our Russia desk intercepted a signal from Moscow. It was transmitted through international commercial networks, specifically to the UK, heavily encrypted. We have prioritised our resources to decipher it; I'm afraid it will take some time, but we are sure that the signal is to activate Brown Bear. We have no more detailed information at this point, but Brown Bear was the acronym of a covert Russian cell operating in the UK five years ago; MI5 were heavily involved in the file at that time."

The MI5 member, Nigel Phillips, nodded.

"We know that one of the Russian covert cells in this country operated under the alias Brown Bear. At the time, we were concerned about activity around strategic areas, for example, unusually high traffic through the GIUK gap. We haven't identified the size or threat posed by this new information but have identified two 'sleeper' names from our previous work which we were monitoring round the clock. Unfortunately, two years ago, we disbanded the surveillance due to inactivity."

Grace Armstrong interjected, "GCHQ has intercepted a file that directly affects us and so now we must put this together with other worrying events and ensure we are prepared. What does the signal say? What and where is this cell Brown Bear? What is it up to?" She paused. "Sir Mark."

Sir Mark had been in the post of Chief of Staff for the UK armed services for over two years; a craggy-faced veteran, he exuded authority and now examined the papers in front of him, adjusting them into a meticulous pattern of squares.

"I'll be brief," he said. "Russian aircraft, ships and even submarines probing our territorial space is not new. We're looking at one or two incursions every single month. For example, last Saturday, six RAF fighter jets were scrambled when Russian aircraft were detected heading towards British airspace.

"On that occasion, six Typhoons, from the air force's Quick Reaction Alert programme, were deployed in pairs. Two of them were dispatched from RAF Lossiemouth in Moray in north-east Scotland, while the third pair flew from RAF Coningsby in Lincolnshire. The first two pairs approached the aircraft before withdrawing, while the third pair finished the job of forcing them to change course.

"One of the intruding aircraft was identified to be a Tupolev Tu-95 Bear, used both as a strategic bomber and long-range maritime patrol plane. This is a routine response to Russian aircraft approaching UK airspace and is coordinated with several other NATO allies. At no point did these aircraft actually enter UK sovereign airspace."

He paused, then went on.

"It's not only UK airspace that is targeted. Last summer, RAF fighter jets were deployed several times to see off Russian planes encroaching on Estonian airspace. At the time, RAF personnel had been participating in Operation Azotize, a four-month deployment in the Baltic country, to support the NATO Baltic air-policing mission. So, this a regular, almost routine, procedure and, while well rehearsed by both sides, is wide open for an accident; it takes only one misstep…"

The home secretary interjected. "Let's be clear, Sir Mark, what is the situation if the intruder does not back off?"

"Emphatic radio demands, coupled with urgent notice to Moscow. Warning shots."

"And if that doesn't work?"

"The engagement orders are clear, which is to harass, until instructions from the Quick Reaction command are received."

The chancellor asked, "Are we clear about the line of communication here?"

"Unauthorized intrusion of sovereign airspace is a significant violation of international law."

"Not quite what I asked, Sir Mark."

"The authority to deliberately to shoot down a sovereign foreign aircraft could only come from the top," Sir Mark hedged.

The home secretary persisted. "Is there a contingency to assume such authority once a line is crossed?"

"It would be a dramatic situation. Too early, and we'd be hauled before every international court, plus the likelihood of starting a war. Too late and the whole point of interception would be lost, with the danger that the intruder is able to accomplish his mission."

"So, we would never actually take the intruder out of the sky?"

Grace Armstrong, catching a glance from Sir Mark, butted in.

"It is a judgement call. Depending on the threat level, we would respond accordingly. But gentlemen, we are digressing from the purpose of this meeting. Sir Mark."

Sir Mark nodded. "The important issue is detecting when that threat level requires a response. It is not only our local patch that is receiving this attention. Last month, Russian and Chinese warplanes flew in tandem in airspace over the Sea of Japan in an intentional, carefully planned manoeuvre designed as a challenge to the United States' Indo-Pacific Strategy."

"Thank you, Sir Mark." The PM was keen to press on. There was a pause; she spoke into the silence.

"This is all very intangible. But I am concerned that we should all be aware of this activity. I want you to quietly step up the readiness of your departments to deal with any contingency."

Her analytical mind, sharpened over years heading up biochemistry research, went on. "This meeting remains confidential; I do not want to start a hare running, and I do not want to see apocalyptical headlines in the tabloids tomorrow! It is important that we all have a political and defence spatial awareness of the wider implications. I want us to put together a covert team to find out what the Russians are trying to do." She looked at Nigel Phillips.

"Nigel, I think MI5 is the right department to lead?"

"Yes, PM, both we and MI6 have files on this – uh, Brown Bear. I'm happy that MI5 take the lead; in fact, I already have a name in mind to head up the team. He was team leader when we first encountered Brown Bear several years ago. Currently, he is employed away from the department, in a consultancy role."

Grace Armstrong said, "Right, we'll go from there and convene a further COBRA when we have something more tangible."

She closed the file in front of her.

"What is the name of the team leader?"

"His name," said Nigel Phillips, "is Matthew Loader."

CHAPTER 3

The day Loader drove north, it was cloudy and cold. He had been invited to stay at the Newby residence overnight.

'Head north out of London,' Newby had said, 'take the M11, change to the A10 and make for Kings Lynn. I'm afraid it's a case of sat nav from there.'

He explained that Loader would enter an Area of Outstanding Natural Beauty. There were a couple of sites awarded Dark Sky Discovery status close by. Newby lived in a farmhouse, well out of sight of rural roads.

"Thank God for sat nav," muttered Loader to himself as he navigated a range of lanes, seemingly criss-crossing and doubling back before finally arriving at Newby's address. There was no house. A tall, wrought-iron gate barred entry to a narrow lane. Loader could see a large property in the distance. Without warning, the gate slowly opened inwards; clearly Loader's arrival was noted on CCTV. He drove along the lane before it opened out into what had been a large farmyard. The house that faced onto the yard was a traditional, mansion-style property with wide steps leading up to the front door. A large barn butting one side of the house made up an 'L' configuration.

Newby was at the door. "The gate's alarmed," he explained. "How was the journey?"

They shook hands; Newby ushered Loader into a hall and through to a spacious living room. It was gracefully furnished; large French windows looked out over a garden and to fields beyond. The room itself had a bookcase against one wall, a TV on the opposite side, while pictures adorned the rest of the wall space. There was a small desk in one corner with a few papers and a laptop. An office chair was askew by the desk. There were two overstuffed armchairs and a settee set at conversational angles.

On one of the chairs was sitting an elegant woman; she stood as they entered.

Newby extended his arm towards her. "My wife, Susan," he said.

Her eyes made warm contact with Loader as he took her hand.

"Matt," he said. "Good to meet you."

Her hand lingered a second or two, slim, smooth. She was fairly tall, with auburn hair, stylishly cut. She wore soft denim trousers, an ivory blouse under a light blue sleeveless jacket. The top three buttons of her blouse were undone, revealing a glimpse of breast snuggling into a lacy bra. Her voice was soft.

"Pleased to see you too. Glad you were able to find us! I hope you had an easy journey from London. George tells me you may be interested in looking into his work."

"Yes, I'm hoping that there is a real story here. I am intrigued, but I warn you, I'm highly sceptical. I may be wasting your time." His smile disarmed the rebuke.

She laughed. "Well, we haven't got any little green men

living here if that's what you mean." She stood aside to let him pass; he caught a whisper of fragrance.

Loader warmed to her. Beneath her smile, he felt there was a hint of loneliness, perhaps sadness.

Newby interjected. "I'll show you to your room, Matt, then a drink and spot of lunch. I'll show you around afterwards."

Over the meal, Newby told him something of his background. Always interested in astronomy from boyhood, he had graduated in astrophysics, going on for his PhD and gaining a position in teaching at the University of Birmingham and later working up to a professorship. Fifteen years ago, he had moved on from observation telescopes to radio astronomy, joining the thousands of enthusiasts across the world who received and analysed universal energy hitting the earth. He moved to Norfolk to build his own radio telescope, hence the remote farm.

As lunch progressed, any reserves fell away and soon the three were engaged in sociable chatter.

"We have a huge barn at the back, which I've made into my 'observatory' and five acres of fields beyond." Newby was obviously keen to get onto the reason for the visit, while Loader, drawn to Susan, was content to extend the meal. He learned that Susan was a professional in her own right. With a PhD in neuroscience, she too had spent much of her time in research. Currently, in a more semi-retired mode, she lectured at the local college. They had no children.

Newby was fidgeting. "Shall we make a start, Matt?"

Loader grinned at Susan. "Can we take a rain check on the washing-up?"

Susan smiled. "I'll hold you to some chores this evening."

Loader followed Newby through a wide hallway and long corridor which led to the barn; he noticed that the connecting door was steel. Newby fiddled with high-security locks.

As they entered, Loader stopped in astonishment.

"Bloody hell, this looks like NASA!"

Newby laughed. "Twenty years of my life is invested here," he said.

The room was huge. All four walls were lined floor to ceiling with equipment racks. There was a door in the corner of the far wall.

"That goes into the other half of the barn, the antenna room," Newby said, catching Loader's gaze.

"I'm speechless." Loader stepped towards a large table in the middle of the room and looked around.

"OK," said Newby, getting serious. "I don't want to be disrespectful, Matt, but how much do you know about radio astronomy?"

"Very little."

Newby grinned.

"So, you get the one-dollar tour. Basically, I'll just tell you what's here, it would take months to get you really on board."

"That's OK with me." Loader was still gazing around with astonishment. He hadn't expected anything like this. Newby moved to the far side of the central table.

"The stuff on this back wall are the receiver amplifiers. They pick up signals from the cosmos from the antenna next door. I'll tell you about that later. The signals are mixed with a local oscillator built on a stable table," he pointed, "to produce an intermediate frequency signal—"

Loader interjected. "Stable table?"

"Yeah, we need an oscillator that is accurate to within sub microwave accuracy, so it needs to be on a platform which cuts out spurious shifts due to ground vibration."

He went on, "The IF signal is passed around to the signal processing bank over there." He indicated the racks of equipment on the left-hand side of the room. "This is where the real work takes place; this is where I analyse and try to extract data." He pointed. "The top rack is a pulse length detector. The next rack down is a pulse recurrence frequency discriminator." He grinned as Loader was about to interrupt. "Don't ask," he quipped and went on. "Below that is a set of phase shift detectors. Don't worry, Matt, you don't need to know. Over there on the other side is a phaser transmitter – I'll explain later," he said again. "Let's look outside at the antenna array."

He opened the door in the far corner of the room which led into the other half of the barn. Loader followed. The roof of the barn had been removed and was open to the elements. On a plinth in the centre of the room stood a large skywards-looking telescope dish. There was little else in the room.

"3.2 metres." Newby anticipated Loader's question. "Look over here." They walked to the far side of the barn. There was a defunct window aperture. Loader looked out over a field, on the far sides of which were stands of trees. Marching across the field were three rows of what looked like telegraph poles; a network of wires stretched between the poles.

"That's where I started," said Newby. "That's a remnant of a wide field antenna array; I went through a phase of building Yagi dipole arrays, then eventually, as I focused more and more on microwaves and trying to measure any pattern in cosmic noise, I set up the dish arrangement."

"Explain cosmic noise."

Newby was anxious to get on, but he put on his lecturer's voice. "Cosmic noise is random noise that originates everywhere in space. We can detect it in radio receivers, generally at frequencies above about fifteen megahertz. This is where we need highly directional antennas. Celestial objects like quasars, super dense objects that lie light years from earth, emit electromagnetic waves in a full spectrum, including radio waves. We can also hear the fall of a meteorite in a radio receiver; we call this Cosmic Background Radiation. CMBR for short. The peak is in the microwave range, which is where my research has been."

He turned back towards the large dish. "All the energy that's out there hits us, Matt, light, infrared, radio, neutron waves, the whole spectrum. It's a case of tuning into an area of interest and trying to analyse it. So, let's go back in and I'll show you the results."

Inside, Newby pulled out several A3-size prints and placed them on the large table.

"Right, Matt, this is a printout of microwave cosmic noise over a short period of time. For years I've left the receivers on twenty-four seven , scanning the skies as the earth rotated. Then, ten years ago, I found out something that made my nerves tingle. I found a specific pattern as the dishes passed the same spot every twenty-four hours as the earth rotated. The difficulty was trying to return to pinpoint that precise same spot every twenty-four hours. Then, once I had stabilised the direction, I discovered an anomaly in the signals coming from that specific point."

He paused. "Matt, to cut a long story short, I found that from that very specific point in the sky was a phase shift in the signal pattern – same place, same time – so I spent months trying to expand it and analyse it. That's when I discovered..." he paused, then for dramatic effect, spaced his words emphatically, "...the... phase... shift... occurred... in... precisely... an... arithmetical... progression."

He stopped, drew a deep breath, then, "This phase shifting indicates intelligence! Matt, you have no idea how awesome it was! I literally felt the hairs on the back of my neck curling. Of course, I immediately thought, what other explanation could there be? The signals could be corrupted by some mundane source: satellites, storms or terrestrial interference; aircraft, even domestic sources. In the end, I had no choice but to accept that these signals were genuine and that they came from a point source in space."

Newby's drama was catching.

Loader was becoming overwhelmed by the atmosphere created by Newby. He had questions, dozens, but Newby pressed on. He placed an oscilloscope printout on top of the pile of drawings. It looked like a blow-up version of the first drawing.

"Look!" he said urgently. "Here." He jabbed his finger on the drawing. "A phase shift. And here another phase shift, and here! Here!" He moved his finger dramatically along the chart.

Loader tried to follow. "OK. I see what you're trying to show me, but how does that indicate intelligence?"

"Don't you see!" Newby almost shouted. "Look at the first one, a phase shift, then nothing. Further along, two phase shifts, then nothing. Further along, three phase shifts, then nothing. Then four phase shifts! Matt, it's an arithmetical progression! One, two, three, four, it's the same every night!"

Loader tried to get his head around what Newby was saying. He understood what Newby told him, but there must be a flaw somewhere, some mundane explanation.

"OK, George. Let's say for a moment this stuff is genuine, why don't you pass it on to the astronomical professionals? Why have you found it and they haven't? They have huge resources and could verify it. You'd be famous."

"*No!*" Newby was emphatic. "I wanted to prove beyond doubt that these were intelligent signals before I made myself look naive and a fool. I was not ready to share my findings. So that's when I built the transmitter; he indicated the bank of equipment on the sidewall. I built a transmitter which mimicked the received signal but shifted the frequency slightly and replaced the phase shift picture patterns with a different progression – two, four, eight, sixteen – and transmitted it back along the same sight line."

Loader was intrigued. "And?"

"Well, nothing. I didn't really expect a result. I just continued the transmissions and got on with other research in-between my lecturing at Birmingham. I told no one."

There was a long silence while Loader digested what Newby had told him. Then, "Let me understand what you have said. You discovered this anomaly ten years ago! You believed it was intelligence from somewhere in the cosmos; you built a transmitter and sent out corresponding signals for over eight years, so I'm still not sure where we are going on all this?"

"Ha ha," shouted Newby, pacing agitatedly. "This was when I decided to come to see you, Matt. A month ago, I got a reply!"

He stopped abruptly; there was silence for a whole minute.

Loader said quietly, "Go on."

"The incoming signal changed from the original progression, and don't forget it had been the same for years, to a more advanced arrangement that could only have been the result of receiving my transmissions – look."

He produced another A3 printout; it looked a similar noise waveform, but parts were quite dark.

"That's the changed pattern, see? A long stream of where the phase changes before a gap, then repeat."

"So, what does it say?"

"Thirty!"

Loader looked blank. "And that's good?"

"Yes, yes, of course! A stream of thirty phase shifts. Thirty is the sum of my transmitted sequence! Don't you see?" He looked at Loader triumphally. "After that, the waveform goes berserk; I have no idea what it means. This is partly why I need the £600,000. Now I've got the sequences saved, I am going to have to get some software muscle in to help decode it."

After spending another two hours discussing the findings, Loader was still unable to accept the results. Newby went over the whole background again.

Susan joined them. "Supper is about ready." She smiled, coming in to look at the papers strewn over the table.

"Did you find any green men, Matt?" Loader laughed, her nearness unsettling him.

Newby was still fired up with his discussion. "You go on in, Matt," he said. "I've got to tidy up a few things here. Get a drink; I'll be along shortly."

Matt returned with Susan, along the hallway into the living room.

"Come on through into the kitchen; I'll fix drinks."

Loader, glass of wine in hand, stood at the centre island worktop.

"Where do you fit in on George's project?" he asked conversationally.

"Nowhere really." She laughed. "I act as a good sounding board – I mean, I know what he's talking about and try to make sensible comment."

"If what George believes is right, it will be earth shattering."

"Well, yes, that is one reason he keeps everything to himself until he is sure. Maybe now is the right time to go public; money is becoming an issue. George wants to get in a software code writer, and finances are difficult…" She left the sentence hanging.

"You said earlier that you worked in Ely?"

"Yes, at the moment I am just trying to keep the finances afloat. It's not what I am used to. I've got a PhD in neuroscience and would prefer to be in a bigger research environment."

"Well, maybe when this breaks, you will be able to change tack."

They were standing around one corner of the worktop, separate but close enough for Loader to sense her fragrance.

He paused and glanced at her; she seemed more fragile than he had noticed, even wistful. He felt an overriding desire to comfort her, from what? The moment passed as she laughed gently. "Maybe," she said. "I'd like to get back to my research project." Before Loader could ask her to expand on that, they heard Newby locking the barn door and entering the living room.

"We're in here, in the kitchen," called Susan. "We're on wine," she added, as Newby appeared. Supper was a straight forward cottage pie with broccoli and carrots.

Newby couldn't help continuing the conversation about the radio signals. Loader maintained interest but, catching a wistful look on Susan's face, he tried to change the subject, and the meal progressed with social trivia.

At 10pm, as Loader was about to suggest calling it a night, his mobile rang. "Excuse me, I've got to take this," he said, the cliche of modern life.

"Loader," he said into the phone.

He listened for a moment, then said in a clipped voice. "Yes, this is Matt Loader."

The caller uttered three letters, "RTB."

"Understood," he said, closing the phone.

"George, Susan, I'm so sorry. I have to get back to London tonight."

Both Susan and Newby chorused their disappointment. As Loader retrieved his overnight case from the bedroom, Newby put together a file of information about the research.

"Matt, this remains confidential until we agree terms. Eh?"

"Of course, I am going to study the facts again and, if we go forward, I'll work out the best way to publish it.

Meanwhile, I do need you to produce more evidence to prove that the transmissions are not faked or somehow terrestrial."

They shook hands; Susan accepted a hug from Loader, her fragrance lingering with him.

"I'll give you a call to arrange another get-together in a couple of days."

CHAPTER 4

Driving back to London, Loader tried to push Newby's project to the back of his mind, but it was impossible. What Newby had uncovered was mind-blowing, with possibly serious consequences for the world. He realised that he was, now, the sole person in the world with the story; the ramifications were huge, going way beyond mere publication in a daily newspaper. How should he cope with the information? One thing was certain: he needed to get back to the farmhouse and query Newby's data in much more detail.

The instruction RTB had been given after the caller received Loader's response 'yes, this is Matthew Loader', thus establishing a voice recognition positive ID.

RTB was an instruction: Return to Base. Loader knew that a second instruction would come once he returned to London. Back in his apartment.

He tried to imagine what was coming. His work as a defence and security correspondent for the *Daily Telegraph* masked his life as a deeply covert senior agent of MI5.

Something had triggered a recall!

It was nearly 1am before Loader climbed into bed; he slept soundly until 6.30am and was showered and dressed by 7.30am. The call came at 8.30am.

"Hi, Matt." It was Jan, the PA to the chief editor of the *Daily Telegraph*.

"Sorry to catch you early, but I've just been told that there is a press briefing at the RUSI at noon. Can you make it?"

Jan had innocently set up Loader's next instruction, time and venue.

"Hi, Jan. Yes, I can make it. What's on?"

"Don't know," she responded. "The brief mentioned something about Britain considering linking up with Asian NATO. Whatever that means."

Loader laughed.

"Well, we'll soon find out, Jan. Tell the press coordinator that I'll be there."

"OK, Matt, anything else?" She made it sound like an invitation.

Loader had not visited his MI5 office in Vauxhall Cross for some years. His deeply covert status meant taking no chances of being seen anywhere near the SIS Building on Albert Embankment. Instead, his communication with 'the office' was through clandestine meetings held in venues in which he could legitimately attend in his role as a newspaper defence correspondent.

In this case, he had been summoned to a meeting to be held in the Royal United Services Institution (RUSI) building in Whitehall.

Sure, there would be a press briefing of some sort, but

the real reason for his recall would be made clear.

The press room was filling up as Loader arrived. The briefing was to be given by the foreign secretary.

The UK was poised to join an informal grouping of US, Australian, Japanese and Indian nations to form a military alliance to counterbalance China's growing influence in the area.

Loader looked around at the newspaper hacks and other Whitehall staff lining up in an untidy semicircle round the foreign secretary.

He saw Nigel Phillips among the crowd, Senior Agent, MI5. His boss.

When the meeting concluded, Loader followed Phillips out of the room and along a corridor to a small office.

Inside, they sat down and exchanged a few pleasantries, and then Phillips placed a file in front of Loader.

"It seems that your old case has resurfaced," he said.

Loader opened the file and quickly scanned the contents. "This file was closed four years ago," he observed.

"Yes. After the cell went dormant. We know the leader and several agents went back to Russia; two of his henchmen remained here and blended into the local background. Victor Ivanov was the number two; he settled in Birmingham. The other, Mikhail Popov, has been tracked to Reading. Surveillance was lifted two years ago after a year of nil reports."

Loader looked at the mugshots again. Both men were in their thirties, dark stubble faces, medium build.

"So, what's brought them back to the fore?"

"Nothing specific, but a week ago, Cheltenham intercepted a signal which activated Brown Bear."

"And that was my case at the time!"

"Quite. We assumed that Brown Bear had been wound down, but perhaps it was just put to sleep. Anyway, it's with us again and in light of deteriorating world affairs, it's crucial that we pick it up."

"OK. I'll get myself up to date."

"Good. It seems to have become urgent. I've assigned you a partner – Bob Dixon – you've worked with him before."

"Yeah, he's a grafter; I'm happy with that."

"Good. The two of you set up a team. I'll leave the size and shape to you. Normal covert recruitment applies, work through AG6. This all stems from a COBRA last Wednesday; you're now in the loop. I've arranged for you to get down to Cheltenham for a briefing – your contact will be Margaret Dibden; she is the head of research and senior desk officer on this case."

"HoR, crikey, big guns."

Phillips grimaced. "Yeah, right. The PM is itsy about the situation. She is looking for answers yesterday."

Loader leaned back in his chair, placing his hands behind his head, stretching.

"Righto. Normal comms?"

Phillips grinned. "Yes. If you could map out something for a COBRA update, not sure when that will be, but we need to be prepared, full stop. Oh, and you're now on the distribution list!"

"OK. I'll get down to Cheltenham. Meanwhile, I'll put out an APB on those two characters," he tapped the file, "and check they are still around."

That evening, back in his apartment, Loader looked at the file. It was 8pm. He was tired but still needed to complete the day's work.

He took a ready meal from the freezer, placed it in the microwave. Pouring a glass of wine, he sat at the kitchen table and opened the Brown Bear file to revise the old case.

At the time, uncovering a large covert Russian cell in the UK had created frenzied activity across both police and security services.

Combined security activities uncovered the identities of over twenty-five Russian spies. Their purpose in the country was unclear. Matters came to a head when one of the officers working for the British intelligence agencies was poisoned. It caused a major response from the UK Government, including a series of punitive measures against Russia and the expulsion of a number of diplomats. The UK response was supported by several countries and, altogether, over one hundred Russian diplomats were expelled from their posts.

Loader, the lead MI5 agent, had identified a covert cell operating under the code name Brown Bear which, following the incident, suddenly went cold. Only two East Europeans who were thought to be associated with Brown Bear remained in the UK; the rest were known to have left the country.

After a further six months' investigation, the file was closed.

Loader finished reading the old files with a sigh; his evening was not finished. He still had to write up the result of the RUSI briefing to cover his presence there.

Opening his laptop, he wrote an article summarising

the conclusions of the RUSI meeting. There was not a word about Brown Bear, nor Newby's startling news.

Loader emailed the article through to Jan, then took the M4 out of London towards Gloucestershire and Cheltenham.

The next day, a piece appeared in the *Daily Telegraph* under Loader's name, describing Britain's intention to join the Asian coalition and included Britain's proposal to expand the G7 into a bigger group of democracies.

CHAPTER 5

GCHQ is the UK's national intelligence, security and cyber agency, charged with keeping the country safe by providing communications and cyber support to government agencies. Spread over five national sites, its headquarters is a sprawling, iconic complex, affectionately known as the Doughnut on the west side of Cheltenham.

Loader arrived at the site mid-morning. Checking in, he was ushered to a small conference room. There was coffee and biscuits provided on a side table. The head of research, Margaret Dibden, arrived and greeted him warmly. They were joined by Adrian Boyce, a senior analyst.

After introductions over coffee, the three made general conversation about their roles, although Loader was careful about how much he said, they were soon on first-name terms.

Margaret opened a file.

"It's very interesting that Brown Bear is already in the domain. I didn't know this until Nigel Phillips brought it out at COBRA." She paused. "Anyway, on the 6th, we intercepted a message from Moscow; it came over the normal commercial satellite communication network to their embassy in London. It would have gone into an internal drop box number automatically rerouted onto pay-as-you-go mobile, practically untraceable, to where, we don't know.

"We captured the message in its entirety – needless to say, it is heavily encrypted. We got the opening gambit that it related to activation of Brown Bear, but the body of the file is taking longer to decode. Adrian is our senior analyst on the job."

Loader asked, "Is it likely that it will be decoded?"

Adrian said, "Oh yes, I expect so; I hope we'll get there. It's sixth-generation encryption, which won't make it easy." Loader looked enquiringly.

Adrian went on.

"The content is not only double encrypted, with scrambled packet switching, but I'm sure that when we get to it, we'll find it needs a destination code to unscramble. This could be a recipient or real-time unlock. In which case, we are in for a long slog, if we can do it at all."

Loader grimaced. "So really the ball is in our court 'til then. We'll have to come from behind and pick up from our old files on Brown Bear."

Margaret said, "We'll continue to work with you on this. What we really need to do is to get to the destination of the message."

They spoke for a further hour on the problem and the tactics going forward.

Back in London, Loader picked up messages from the Thames Valley Police and the Birmingham Police Authority.

The Russian Victor Ivanov had disappeared off the radar. A trawl was being made of the Birmingham registers, but it looked as if Ivanov had left the area with no trace of his onwards destination.

There was better luck with the Thames Valley Police. They confirmed that a man fitting the description and name of Mikhail Popov was still residing in their area in the suburb of Reading. There was no record of any law-breaking activity.

Loader contacted Nigel Phillips. "We've located one of the sleepers from the Brown Bear file. We can make a start there, see if there are still any connections."

"OK, what do you want?"

"To start with, I am going to put a twenty-four seven on the guy, name of Mikhail Popov. I want another in the team – twenty-four seven is too much for one over a period – and I want to set up a vantage point. There is an empty property within sight of Popov's address; I'll arrange with Thames Valley to take it over pro tem. That will do for starters, see where it takes us."

Nigel Phillips agreed. "Right. A female would be good? Make like a couple."

"OK. Thanks, Nigel. I'll follow up on the missing guy. Meanwhile, I'll sort out some details with Dixon."

CHAPTER 6

Loader called Newby and set off to Norfolk. This time he told Newby he would stay overnight but leave directly after breakfast.

Both Newby and Susan greeted him at the farmhouse door. They met as old friends; Newby gave Loader a man hug. Susan happily embraced Loader. "Good to see you again," she said softly.

Loader could see that they were both bursting to tell him something.

"You've found something out," he said.

"Well, we both have!" Newby was almost incoherent with eagerness. "I found another aberration in the signal pattern, but it was Susan who interpreted it. I was going through some recordings of the last few weeks of receiver noise and discovered a change in the sequence, again followed by continuous noise, with no pattern that I could detect." He paused dramatically. Loader waited. Newby went on. "The original arithmetic progression was still there, but the second set, that transmitted by me, was repeated back to us with the third figure – thirty – in the middle! That's different."

Loader looked puzzled. "So, what is the significance? The signal got a bit garbled somehow."

"No, no. Think about it. Look, nine years ago, I detected the arithmetic sequence: one, two, three, four. Within a year, I had built my transmitter and responded with a different sequence: two, four, eight, sixteen. Then, two months ago, I detected a new sequence: thirty phase shifts all equidistant, thirty being the sum of my transmitted pattern. OK so far?"

Loader nodded. "Yes, I got all that."

"Right, this latest detected sequence is: two, four, thirty, eight, sixteen."

"OK," said Loader dubiously.

Newby stared at Loader with evangelical fervour. "It was Susan who came up with the result, didn't you, Susan?"

They both looked at her. "Well, it's only a theory, really," she said quietly. "The only language that works without learning is maths. Here, their transmission – thirty – sits in the middle of ours, two, four, thirty and then eight, sixteen. They are thirty; we are two, four, eight, sixteen; they are in the middle of our sequence."

"And?" Loader asked, still puzzled.

"I think," Susan said carefully, "it means that the aliens are coming to us!"

There was a stunned silence; Newby and Susan waited.

Loader stood up, paced the floor.

"For God's sake, Susan. That's a stretch. You are talking science fiction here. How the hell can I present this as a serious finding?"

Susan looked vulnerable; Loader immediately felt apologetic, an urge to comfort her with a hug.

Instead, he said, "Look, we need to start again. Go over everything. Perhaps we can present the facts as you've proven and leave out the conclusion."

Newby looked deflated. "As soon as that is published, the conclusions will follow and others will get the credit. This has been nearly twenty years of my life, Matt."

"Yes, sure, I understand. Look, let's just take a step back. Go over all the details again. I am still worried you are being hoaxed in some way, and that would be disastrous. Please, George! Double-check that every dot and comma can be substantiated by science; let's leave the philosophy for a moment."

Susan looked hurt. Newby rubbed his hands over his head.

"I have checked everything through again, Matt; I swear the signals technically can only come from space. But," he added, "I have got nowhere with the noise following the coded response – the spectrum has gone berserk; I cannot make head nor tail of it."

Loader felt more pangs of doubt. "What I don't understand is why this activity hasn't been picked up by the professional astronomers, NASA, for example, or SETI?"

Newby shrugged. "Many discoveries in science, especially astronomy, have been made by amateurs. But I am sure this discovery will be made by someone else any time now." He sounded dejected.

"Right. Here's a plan, George. I've something else on for a couple of days. Use that time to revise everything. Then, when I get back, I'll have a contract, and if everything still stacks up, you'll get the money."

Newby heaved a sigh of relief.

Susan smiled uncertainly.

She had prepared a supper. This time, they sat in the kitchen and chatted over the meal.

CHAPTER 7

Mikhail Popov was totally unaware that he had suddenly become a person of significant interest. He went about his uneventful life as normal. Unmarried, he lived in a small, terraced house whose only merit was being a short walk to the river and the local pub.

At the end of his street, a similar property had its 'For Sale' notice withdrawn, and a couple took up residence. A casual observer would have noticed that the furnishings which arrived by a small pantechnicon were very sparse, but perhaps it was a vanguard of more to come.

Bob Dixon and Dawn Banks were not married to each other or to anyone else, but they were colleagues who had a good working arrangement and separate bedrooms. From their new living-room window, which looked onto the street, they were able to see the front door of number twenty-five, home of Mikhail Popov.

By the time their few furnishings were distributed, they had ascertained that Popov was at work at a packaging firm a mile away. His car, checked against the DVLA register, was left parked in his short driveway.

Dixon called at number twenty-five. There was no reply, which was expected but a precaution. On leaving, Dixon unobtrusively bent over the front wheel arch of the parked car. There was a slight 'clunk' as a tracking device secured itself magnetically to the underside.

He and Dawn Banks quickly established Mikhail's routine, having already received a short employment file from Thames Valley Police.

They sorted out bedding and kitchen arrangement and set up an array of equipment on a table in the living room. Beside two laptops was the transponder for the tracking device and a monitor receiving CCTV signals from a camera set up to watch the front entrance of the packaging firm.

At the end of the first full day of unobtrusive surveillance, they submitted a 'routine activity' report to Loader in London.

And the next day.

And the next day.

Mikhail led a totally uneventful life. The few people he did talk to were identified and vetted by both the police and the security service.

The third day produced a small burst of activity as he returned from work and got into the old Toyota parked in his drive.

"Subject on move," stated Dixon quietly, speaking into a mobile phone auto dialling to an unmarked police car waiting a street away. He said hastily to Dawn Banks, "I'm on it," grabbing his car keys and leaving the house.

Popov's old Toyota proceeded at a leisurely pace into the town of Reading and on towards the Old Bath Road.

After about five miles, Popov turned into a driveway of a modern half-tiled house. As he got out of the car, a woman emerged from the doorway and welcomed him in a warm embrace. The police car, unnoticed by the couple, went on by, slowing and turning to wait on sentry, fifty yards away. Dixon arrived moments later and joined them. The address and occupant's name would be recorded and checked. The Toyota remained in the driveway overnight. Mikhail got back into the car at 8am and drove leisurely back through Reading and into work.

Loader continued to press Birmingham Police for updates on tracing Victor Ivanov. He checked back with Cheltenham – there was no breakthrough in decoding the Brown Bear files. He set up liaison contacts with the MoD to be informed of changes of patterns to UK territorial violations. He discussed the situation with MI5 and set up a review of other 'foreign national persons of interest'.

The eighth day was different.

Popov left home at the normal time, but instead of walking towards his workplace, he got into his car.

"Uh oh. *Bob!*" called Dawn Banks. "Popov's motoring."

She snatched the car keys; Dixon hurried from the kitchen; and they quickly left the house and got into their car.

"Subject on move," stated Dixon quietly, speaking into the mobile phone, auto dialling to the nearby unmarked police car.

They glimpsed the Toyota turning at the end of the street and discreetly followed. Two junctions ahead, the Toyota had right of way over traffic from the right. The police car was waiting. The Toyota went through; Banks, who was driving the MI5 car, slowed, allowing the police car into the stream, taking up tailing position. Banks dropped back, keeping a distance from both cars.

"Subject moving west on M4." Dixon was patched into Loader's London number.

"Subject southbound on A34."

Thirty minutes later. "Subject right, right, westbound A303."

The Toyota seemed in no hurry, just out for a drive.

"Subject left, left, southbound, A343."

"Subject left, left. Unmarked road."

They made two more changes of direction on minor roads. Dixon scrabbled around trying to find the road markings. The Toyota slowed, turning through tall iron gates into a walled estate.

Moments later, the police car passed the entrance and drove on, followed at a distance by Dixon and Banks. They convened about half a mile further on. Dixon's tracker would alert them if the Toyota moved on.

The Toyota remained parked in the large gravel circle in the front of the house for the remainder of the day, finally leaving in the early evening and returning home. The tailing unmarked police car followed at a distance. Dixon and Banks waited for instructions.

In London, Loader received the information and soon had the details of the manor house. The owner was a Max Turner. He lived there with his wife and three staff: housekeeper-cum-cook Emily Johnson, cleaner-cum-maid Doris Blackwell, and the third member was a gardener, or groundsman, as the brief described him.

None showed up on any local or national databases.

CHAPTER 8

Days were passing without much progress on the Brown Bear file. There was no news of the whereabouts of Victor Ivanov, last seen in Birmingham over two years ago.

Mikhail Popov, having been located living in Reading, was leading an apparently blameless and boring life. His one deviation, recorded, a visit to Max Turner, near Salisbury, remained an enigma.

Background searches on Max Turner and wife produced no evidence of a clandestine life.

GCHQ had so far not been able to decipher the Brown Bear activation file. Both MI5 and MI6 filtered data from all known dissident groups, but nothing emerged which would link them to the original Brown Bear activities.

Loader took the opportunity to visit George and Susan Newby in Norfolk again. The main gate to the track leading to the Newby's farmhouse was closed. Loader was expected, and as soon as he called on the intercom, the gate began to open.

"Come on through." It was Susan's voice, sounding warm.

"Thank you, Susan, see you in a min." Loader felt a pang of pleasure in hearing her voice. As he pulled into the front yard, Susan appeared at the door.

They embraced as old friends.

"George had to go into town," she said as she led him into the kitchen. "He'll be back soon."

Loader paused in surprise. A child was at the kitchen island, busy mixing something in a bowl.

"This is my friend Emily," said Susan, going to the girl, drawing her close to her side.

The girl stared warily at Loader.

"Hello, Emily," said Loader, recovering quickly. "I'm Matt."

The girl said nothing.

"Emily and her mum are staying overnight. Emily is keen to look at the stars, so we're waiting until it gets dark and then we'll go and look at the sky through the sighting 'scope." She gave Emily a squeeze. "Let's leave the mixing for a moment, dear, you go and see Mummy in the living room while I talk to Matt and make us a drink."

Emily continued to stare at Loader. He guessed she was about twelve years old; she made no move to leave Susan's side.

"Come on then, Em, I'll come with you; let's go and find Mummy."

She gave Loader a warning shake of the head, leading Emily out of the kitchen.

"Coffee?" she asked on her return, fussing with the coffee machine without waiting for a response. "How was the trip?"

"Thanks. Straight forward really, no hold-ups." Loader

wandered around, then stood on the opposite side of the island table.

"So, how are things going?"

Susan looked across the worktop.

"I first met Emily and her mum Tracey about two years ago. I was doing a research project at Kings, studying cognitive psychology. We went round several hospitals and hospices to chat to patients. I was particularly interested in children's neurology problems, to try and understand the misfunctioning in the brain's formative years.

"When I met these people, the children and the parents, Matt, I was bowled over – the courage, the fear, the camaraderie of those affected – it was so humbling.

"Emily was in the East Anglian Hospice and had been diagnosed with some form of brain disorder at six years old. At first it was treated as a form of dementia – memory loss – problems in constructing sentences, misplacing things and so on.

"When I met them, I could see that her mum, Tracey, was at the end of her tether. She herself had come from a broken home, had Emily in her teens. Her partner ditched her as soon as he knew that Emily was flawed, but you know, Matt? There is a beauty in broken things."

Susan paused, composing herself. "Tracey is a single mum trying to bring up a child with brain damage, with no money, no proper job, no support. It was heartbreaking to take it in. Anyway, we became friends. I visited when I could. Then the final straw came when later tests revealed that Emily had a brain tumour. Apparently inoperable and no cure. Emily is twelve; they do not believe that she will see sixteen."

Susan stopped, tears in her eyes. She twisted the coffee cup around in her hands, trying to compose herself.

Loader took in the pathos, the agony of those experiencing hopeless situations.

Susan topped up the coffee cup and took a deep breath. "Anyway, I got to know Tracey and Emily quite well and, after one evening's visit, I was saying goodbye at the front door when Emily caught my hand and gesticulated to the dark sky. 'Stars,' she said.

"Tracey told me that Emily loves looking at the sky and spends ages looking out of a dark bedroom window into the night. That week, I bought her a child's book on astronomy. She absolutely loved it. Every time I visited after that, she would bring me the book and point to pictures that intrigued her. It was heartbreaking and heart-warming at the same time. I can't explain it, Matt."

"You just did," Loader said gently. They stood in silence for a while. Loader said, "And George?"

"Everything is fine, Matt. George has been a lot more relaxed now that he has your help."

"Well, that's what I need to talk to you both about—"

Susan interjected quickly. "There isn't a problem, is there?"

"No, no, I wanted to sort out what we say, and how we release it to the public, and to go through the basis of a contract."

Susan relaxed.

Loader sipped his coffee. "What are your plans, Susan?"

"Today?"

"No, I mean generally, in the future."

"I haven't thought a lot about the future. The last few months – well, last few years really – have been pretty wearing." She smiled, but Loader detected a wistfulness in her voice.

"Yes, I can believe that. George is pretty much driven by this project, but Susan, if it is all true, he, and you, will be marked down in history. Let's face it, it is the most earth-shattering event ever."

Susan nodded, coffee cup in hand.

Loader went on, gently. "Where do you fit in this mind-boggling project, Susan?"

She was quiet for a moment.

"I've worked with George on this ever since we met up at uni, some twenty years ago. He was already a professor when I graduated; I was infatuated with the philosophy of life and intelligence – even then George was driven to search for evidence of intelligence in the universe – we just seemed to hit it off. In fact, he got me my first job. We worked in the same university for a while.

"Then we married – there is a big age difference – it has been mainly a marriage of convenience. Our scientific interests overlapped. He is the brains behind the astronomy bit; I just help with his analysis – I have my own ideas."

"What are they? Your ideas, I mean."

Susan gave a deprecating shrug. "I started out as a microbiologist. Then became interested in the functioning of the human brain, well, its malfunctioning really. I was studying disruptive diseases such as Parkinson's, Epilepsy, Dementia, ADHD and so on. Anyway, I got my PhD in neuroscience, then took up research at colleges in the early days. Now I have sort of retired; I do lectures and research courses on a supply basis."

"You still lecture?"

"Well, yes. The SGP keeps me fairly busy."

"SGP?"

"Oh! The SGP is an informal group of scientists, mainly neuron but also from psychology and philosophy. It's an international group called Search for the Genesis of the Psyche." She paused.

Loader smiled encouragingly. "Go on."

"Not much else. George has been wrapped up in his project ever since uni days. I had an interest in what he was doing, but my real interest has always been neuroscience, particularly how the human brain functions, how it defines us."

Susan fiddled with her coffee cup.

"Who are we, Matt? We all know about brain cells, neurons, synapses and all that, but there is an energy somewhere in brain cells, our 'self' or 'being' which directs their behaviour. Despite the huge advances made in the study of the brain, no one has come up with an answer. The SGP group believe that there is a 'brain within the brain.'"

"Whew! That's deep, Susan, a bit above my pay scale." He softened his words with a gentle laugh.

He caught a momentary glimpse of evangelical fervour. She relaxed and laughed, slipping back into everyday conviviality.

"And what about you, Matt, what makes you tick?"

He began to shrug disarmingly but, looking across the table into her eyes, he felt a rush of intimacy, their eyes revealing depths unspoken.

"Not a lot to say really," he said. "But in strict confidence, and you must not breathe a word to anyone, even George, but I am not who I seem to be."

For a moment, her eyes studied Matt's face, penetrating, analytical.

"You mean, you really *are* a little green man?"

They both laughed and the spell was broken.

"No, but my job as a correspondent for the *Telegraph* is sort of part-time."

Matt couldn't believe he was letting down his guard so readily. He hastily added, "I sort of work for the Government."

"Ah ha!" Susan exclaimed. "I knew it! I thought you seemed to have a lot more influence than you let on. Tell me what you do, Matt, or is it a big secret?"

"I've said too much already; if I tell you any more, I'll have to kill you," he joked.

"I wouldn't like that," she said solemnly, then smiled and reached out across the table, placing her hand on his. "Your secret is safe with me," she said softly.

They reverted to safer, more general conversation. Loader learned that she had never had children, never been abroad for holidays. George's preoccupation with his search for extraterrestrial intelligence eclipsed normal social activities. It seemed that over the years, Susan had become trapped into a monastic life that eschewed ordinary family life.

"You really ought to take a holiday," he said. "It would do you good to take a break from the intense life here. Somewhere dreamy, in the sun, or say, Verona, take in an opera, Nabucco or something."

Susan learned that Loader had never married. His earlier life included a spell in the army, Special Forces. "Not conducive for married life," he said lightly.

"Is there someone special in your life now?" she asked, adding hastily, "Sorry, I didn't mean to…"

He felt a sudden stupid ache. "No," he said simply, looking at her.

She returned his gaze. In that instant, he knew that she knew and, in confusion, suggested that another coffee would be welcome.

The intimacy was interrupted by a scream from the living room.

They both leapt up and dashed through the hall into the living room.

Emily was standing across the room screaming uncontrollably, her fists clenched and arms pressed rigidly downwards.

A young woman, hardly more than a child herself, was kneeling on the floor collecting the remains of a shattered glass.

She looked up as they entered; Loader saw a face etched in despair and embarrassment.

Susan crossed quickly to Emily and cradled her close, soothing.

Loader knelt beside the young woman and started to pick up shattered shards of glass.

"Hi," he said. "I'm Matt, Susan's friend. You must be Emily's mum."

"I'm so sorry," the girl said in a haunted voice. "It was an accident. I'll pay for the new glass." She was close to tears.

Loader got Tracey to look at him as he smiled gently.

"You will do nothing of the sort. It's not important, Tracey," he said. "I often drop stuff. Please don't think any more about it. Here, come and sit down on the sofa with me."

"I'm so sorry," she repeated.

Loader steered her to the sofa. She sat, dejected, defeated.

"You really must not worry about it," Loader repeated, anxious to find words to assuage the girl's guilt. "These things really do happen all the time."

Emily's screams subsided as Susan continued to cuddle and soothe her.

As she quietened, Susan took her into the kitchen, to the mixing bowl. "Let's finish these scones, shall we?"

Loader sat beside Tracey. He felt at a complete loss to comfort the girl, her face drawn. Slowly, emotions subsided, and Loader was able to distract her into generalities. Her defeated attitude came over strongly. Loader saw the years of worry weighing intolerably on the young girl as they talked. Not for her, the joy of youth, of social interaction, but a drudge of childcare, living hand to mouth and worry for Emily's future.

But slowly she relaxed, and they were able to go into the kitchen to join the others and make a cup of tea.

Pacified, Tracey and Emily returned to the living room. Emily became engrossed in her well-thumbed astronomy book.

Newby returned just as Susan was starting to prepare an early evening meal.

"Hello, Matt, sorry I was out, had to go into town." Newby seemed energised by the prospect of moving his project into his final phase and getting funds to service his debts.

"Tracey and Emily are in the living room," mentioned Susan. "Emily wants to look through the sighting 'scope again."

Newby nodded indifferently; entertaining a child was not his priority. He wanted to hear about progress for support of his project but contained himself as Tracey and Emily appeared in the kitchen.

At the dining table, Loader noticed that Tracey cut Emily's food for her and that Emily ate with a fork clutched in her right hand, her left arm hanging at an odd angle.

Maintaining light conversation was difficult. Newby was clearly anxious to get the meal over with and on to business; Tracey, still embarrassed by the accident, tried to be on her best behaviour, nervously following the conversation; Emily ate her food clumsily, pausing occasionally, her features alternating between an intense stare at Loader or Newby and an unfocused stare into the middle distance; Susan desperately tried to bridge the conversation between everyone.

Loader did his best to engage Tracey in small talk.

By the time the meal was over, it was mercifully growing dusk. Susan suggested that they move into the office for a discussion and that Emily could go into the antenna room. Tracey stayed close to Emily and said she would go into the antenna room with her.

Stepping through the steel door into the 'office', Loader was again awed by the scale of the equipment lining the walls.

Equipment racks covered the walls floor to ceiling. Six large monitors adorned the back wall.

One monitor showed an image of the night sky, a recorded image since it was still dusk. Four monitors showed various 'noise' waveforms racing across the screens. The sixth monitor showed a listing in software code.

The whole room seemed alive with activity; red and green indicator lights showed on many panels and a low hum seemed to pervade the room.

Loader was conscious of electrostatics in the air. He could feel the hairs on the back of his neck and forearms tingle.

They sat around the large central table, moving papers and books aside. Loader took a folder from his briefcase.

After pleasantries, George said, "Everything is OK, isn't it? I mean about getting paid for this."

There was an undercurrent of anxiety in his voice.

Loader was getting the message that the Newbys were strapped for cash and that George needed to spend yet more.

"I have arranged a contract, well, more of an MoU really, with a group of interested parties. What this document does, George, is to offer you an incremental payment for your story. You will be paid an upfront fee of ten per cent of contract value on your signature.

"You must read it carefully before signing; there are several things to note. The most important is that once the technical elements are disclosed, you will no longer have rights or control. The information becomes public information and free for all to use.

"Secondly, the contract is in two parts. One, an initial payment upon submission of your story up to, but not including, details or coordinates of the technical side. Two, a much larger payment upon submission of your full story. This does not include film rights which I have secured as a separate deal."

He paused.

"One final point is that I cannot believe it will be long before the astronomical societies discover what you have, and then you've lost the edge – the contract recognises this. Advance on signing remains, but the final values will be greatly reduced."

He looked across the table. Susan was silent, inscrutable. George stared at the table, drumming his fingers nervously.

"Bottom line, Matt, if I sign here and now?"

Loader held up his hand, three fingers extended. He held his index finger.

"Money payable immediately on signing."

He held the second finger of his extended hand. "Exclusive minimum with my publisher and one other partnered publisher."

He held his third finger. "Same deal for the full monty, bigger sum. And film rights with a UK studio. All in all, we're looking at about £500,000."

George's mind was working overtime.

"So, in time, I could end up with a million?"

"Basically, yes. But the film rights include royalty payments, so it could be a lot more, and," he grinned to lighten the atmosphere, "there are rich pickings from the public speaking circuit – you could even write a book."

There was silence.

Loader glanced at Susan – there were tears in her eyes – he could see the years of cloistered living, of financial hardship weighing on her. He wanted to smile encouragement, but she stared steadfastly at the table, discreetly wiping the corner of her eye.

The moment passed. George was taking deep sighs, his face slowly lightening. He held out his hand for the document; he started to read. Susan got up and quietly left the room.

An hour later, they regrouped in the kitchen. George was relaxed, jovial. Susan looked relieved, joining in the smiles and congratulations. George insisted that they toasted the signing with a glass of wine.

Loader accepted. "But a small one, George. I've another busy day tomorrow."

He looked at Susan; her eyes met his, neutral, giving nothing away, but on taking his leave, he received an embrace that was warmer than usual.

CHAPTER 9

DC David Bashley knocked on the door. "Hello," he said to the unkempt, oldish man who opened the door.

"My name is DC Bashley." He proffered his ID card as proof. "I wonder if you could help me – I'm enquiring about the previous occupant, Victor Ivanov."

"Dunno, mate, never heard of him."

"You never saw him?"

"Nah, the place was empty when we moved in, sorry, mate."

"Was there any post to forward to him?"

The man scrunched his face. "Nah, nothing like that."

"Did anyone ever call after you moved in, asking for him?"

"Nah."

The conversation was clearly going nowhere.

"Right, well, thank you for your help." The slight sarcasm was lost on the man.

Bashley drove off to the district council tax office.

Doris was the office manager, pleasant with a helpful nature. She was comfortable in her role.

"Victor Ivanov," she repeated, keying into her desktop computer. "Ah yes, here's his address, Holland Road, tax band B. He no longer lives there."

David Bashley smiled in appreciation.

"Is there a forwarding address?"

"No – we don't have that information, uh…"

"David," DC Bashley provided.

"I'm Doris," she said.

"What about bank details?"

Again, consultation with the computer. "Yes, paid direct debit. Lloyds Bank."

"That's great. Can you let me have the account details? I'll get onto them. Police matter." He laughed. "Saves me having to arrest you."

The next day, Bashley visited the local branch of Lloyds Bank and introduced himself to the manager, who was helpful but no help.

"Account closed," he said. "July last year."

"OK. That's about when he moved away. Any forwarding address?"

"No, I'm afraid not."

"What about the transfer of the final balance?"

"No good there either." The manager sounded apologetic. "The balance was withdrawn before closing."

"Well, I guess that's it then. Thanks for your help."

Bashley sat in the car park for a time, musing, then pulled into the traffic and headed towards a petrol forecourt that was nearest to Holland Road. He identified himself to the attendant at the cash desk and held up a photo of Ivanov. "Have you any memory of this person coming here to buy fuel?"

The attendant studied the photo. "No, I can't say that I recognise him. Mind you, we get a fair few people through here every day."

"He was local; I thought he might be a regular."

"Sorry, can't help."

"What about CCTV? Do you have the recordings?"

The man brightened up. "Well, yes, we do."

"How far back do you keep them?"

"Three months, it's pretty standard."

"Damn! This man would have left the area just before that."

Bashley thanked the man and got into his car, driving back towards Holland Road.

Ahead of him, on the pavement, was a woman walking towards him, pushing a baby buggy. He drew up alongside her.

"Hi. Can you tell me where the nearest corner shop is, please?"

"Sure," she said. "Carry on the way you are going 'til the junction, turn left, then first right. There is a SPAR convenience store on the corner."

Bashley thanked the woman and drove on, following her instructions.

He parked near the shop. Inside, he identified himself yet again to the assistant behind the counter.

"Do you recall ever serving this man?" he asked, offering the photo of Ivanov.

"Oh yes. He used to come in here often but moved away a few months ago."

Bashley's pulse quickened. "Do you know where he went?"

"No, he never said. I didn't really know him – he was a fairly taciturn type – but he did seem to hit it off with Greta."

"Greta?"

"Yes, she's the other girl working here."

"Perhaps she could help me. Can I speak with her?"

"Sorry, sir, she left a couple of weeks ago. Sad to lose her, she was a good worker and nice too."

Bashley was deflated. "Where did she go?"

"I don't know." Then, thinking a moment, added, "She did mention something about Norfolk."

"Do you by any chance have a photo of her?"

"Not really; we weren't friends or anything. There is a staff picture that Richard took at our Christmas do."

"Richard?"

"He's our manager." She rummaged in a drawer under the till. "Here you are."

Bashley took the photo. There were six grinning faces, four girls, two men.

"That's Greta," the assistant said, pointing to one of the faces, dark hair closely tied back.

"Fantastic," Bashley said. "Can I borrow it and get a copy made?"

"Sure, no problem. Is she in trouble?"

"No. Not at all. We just want to ask her a few questions. What did you say her surname was?"

"I didn't. It's Adamik."

"Well, thank you. You have been a great help."

Bashley bought a snack bar, got back into his car, musing over the photo as he ate, then drove back to the police station. In his office, he looked up Norfolk on his road atlas. Then, following a discussion with his DI, he called Norfolk Constabulary.

CHAPTER 10

Loader's mobile phone rang. It was Susan Newby in a near hysterical state.

"Matt," she said urgently. "We've had a break-in; George has gone!"

"What do you mean 'gone'! What happened, are you OK?"

"Yes, I'm alright, Matt." Susan was close to tears. "I was out. When I came home, the front door was open; George's office had been torn apart, papers everywhere, and there was no sign of George."

"Have you called the police?"

"No, I called you."

"Are you sure you're alright?"

"Yes, yes. I'm a bit frightened."

Loader pictured her at the phone, calling, vulnerable; he had a desire to comfort her.

"Susan," he said firmly. "Everything will be alright. Listen carefully. Do not touch anything. I will contact the local police; they will be with you very soon. When they come, make sure they give you a password before you let them in, say – uh – 'Bear'. They will be special police and will guard everything until I get there."

"Are you going to come up?"

"Of course, Susan. I will be with you shortly. Now, get yourself a cup of tea and wait for the police. Remember – 'Bear'. Otherwise, keep the door locked."

"OK, Matt." She sounded tremulous, relieved.

"Don't worry, I'll be there soon."

Disconnecting, Loader immediately keyed in a new number.

"DCI's office," a voice answered.

"DCI Weston please."

"Putting you through now, sir."

Loader explained the situation and requested immediate assistance. "I've told Mrs Newby to lock herself in; I am on my way there now. Use password 'Bear.'"

His next call was to Battersea Heliport.

"Code XP-2112, helicopter available now?"

"Can do. Destination?"

"Just north of Norwich."

"ETD?"

"I'll be with you in twenty minutes!"

An hour later, the helicopter circled Newby's farmhouse, landing in the rear paddock.

He was met at the front door by an armed police officer. As Loader identified himself, Susan rushed into the hall.

"Matt!" she cried, running into his arms.

Loader hugged her. 'It'll be OK," he soothed. Later, over a coffee, they discussed the events.

"Why?" She asked. "Why would anyone rob us here? You haven't published anything yet, have you?"

"No, not at all. But we need to find out what they could have taken and how much of George's work could get into the public domain."

"And where's George?"

"Of course. The police forensic team are on their way. Once they have looked around, we must try to assess the possibilities. Did they get into the barn?"

"No. I don't know if they tried, but the door is still locked."

"What about the radio telescope equipment, does it need attention?"

"No, it runs twenty-four seven, has done for years, ever since George locked onto the coordinates. There is equipment recording the receiver signals – I don't know how much it stores."

"Probably on a loop of a week or something," said Loader. "OK, let's just leave that side alone for now. We've got enough on to find out where George has got to."

Susan had prepared an evening meal. The forensic team spent a short time in the office but had little to report.

Over supper, Loader tried to set out a plan. He had arranged a permanent surveillance of the farm. The subject of George's absence was a police matter and would be followed up by the local police force. Loader had spoken to the DI in charge of the investigation and warned him of the security services' involvement.

Susan toyed with her food. "What do you think has happened to George?" she asked.

"Well, he could have left for some reason voluntarily, on some mission, unlikely though," Loader said, "given the state of the office. We have to assume that he went unwillingly."

He hesitated. "We must be prepared that this work could find its way into the public domain, in which case we have to expect to be invaded by hordes of press hacks. Keep the roadside gate shut, Susan, and vet who comes in."

They talked until late. Loader spent some time on the phone.

"Susan, I have meetings tomorrow that I cannot get out of, I'll get back as soon as I can, meanwhile, the police will be going through the missing persons routine. I've arranged some company for you, a female plain clothes police officer and a local guard too."

Susan looked crestfallen. "I understand, Matt. You seem to have a lot more involvement with the authorities than I imagined."

"Well, I am a defence and security correspondent," he quipped gently, turning the subject aside.

"I'll be back soon, Susan, and we'll get to the bottom of it all, together."

"Thank you, Matt, it's good of you," she said simply. It was 1am before they parted to their bedrooms.

The next morning at 9am, the helicopter returned, bringing the plain clothes officer, who ducked under the rotating blades towards Loader.

"Hello. Julie Hammond, Close Protection Officer, Met," she shouted above the engine noise.

Loader escorted her from the landing area, carrying her overnight bag; he briefed her on the situation, noting, discreetly, a slight bulge below her jacket on the hip. She was armed.

In the house, over coffee, as they discussed routine, he said, "I want you to take great care of Susan – don't let her out of your sight, twenty-four seven."

Events were pressing in on him, but he had to leave. He embraced Susan, telling her to be strong; he would be back ASAP. Holding her close, he took in her fragrance, her gentleness and her fear. He felt unsettled, holding her for longer, wanting to stay.

He boarded the helicopter. He was going to Salisbury.

CHAPTER 11

Loader was frustrated. Opening up the Brown Bear file was getting nowhere. He had only the two names to look into: Popov and Ivanov.

GCHQ had so far not come up with any new information.

Ivanov had disappeared off the radar.

Popov continued to lead his uneventful life in Reading, except for the one visit to Max Turner in Wiltshire – what was that about?

Perhaps it was time to examine this more closely.

Policing in the area of Max Turner's manor house came under the jurisdiction of the Wiltshire Police.

DCI Gibson was nominated to coordinate police intelligence in the area and arranged with Loader, through MI5, to set up an incident room in the Amesbury police station.

Continued surveillance of Popov in Reading was handed over to Thames Valley Police. Dixon and Banks moved their centre of operations into the Amesbury area. Loader called a meeting with the new incident group. DC Bashley joined them from Birmingham.

After introductions, Loader began. "Let's start off by summarising what this operation is all about. A month ago, GCHQ picked up a Russian signal, activating a covert Special Ops Russian team here in UK, code name Brown Bear. This group has been known about for some years but went off the radar two years ago, deemed to have been disbanded. Surveillance was dropped due to inactivity and the files closed.

"Some of the operatives were recorded as returning to Russia. Two were last known to have settled in the UK. One of them, Ivanov, whereabouts unknown, was last recorded as settling in Birmingham. DC Bashley here is chasing this up and has promising leads. The other, Popov, was found in Reading. Thames Valley, together with Bob and Dawn here, have been watching Popov's movements. Nothing unusual until last Wednesday when Popov made a trip into this area, to a large manor house off the A303. The owner, a Max Turner, is, to all intents and purposes, legit."

Loader paused for a moment, then continued. "So, what's the operation about? Well, GCHQ are still trying to decipher the signal from Moscow, but it has raised concerns in government as the timing coincides with a fairly rapid increase in excursions by Russian assets into both UK and Baltic sovereign areas, both sea and airspace. This pattern is being replicated by the Chinese, who are building up a formidable force and also carrying out expansionary excursions towards Taiwan.

"The Cabinet think tank does not have any tangible evidence to cause specific alarm, but the PM, who thinks well outside the box, has asked for examination of the implications of the Russian activation of Brown Bear. She wants to ensure that UK intelligence has examined every scenario possible and doesn't get blindsided.

"To summarise. This is very much a covert surveillance operation to find out the reasoning for activation of the Russian operation Brown Bear. The only start we've got is that two Brown Bear agents are still residing in the UK. Meanwhile, we are waiting for GCHQ to unravel the signal. What does it say? Who received it? Is there a threat to the UK that we're not seeing? Not much to go on yet.

"I'm puzzled! Popov and Turner. I don't understand what these two have in common. Popov is clearly a low-level stores assistant. Max Turner is by all accounts a wealthy businessman, with no criminal record." He paused.

"What is a known Russian sleeper doing visiting a successful English businessman in his home? I think we need to find out more about Mr Turner."

He paused, then held up a paper.

"I've put a copy of this in your file," he said as everyone leafed through the papers in front of them. "As you see, Max Turner and his wife are sole directors of a nationwide firm of couriers. Their main depot is in Basingstoke, but they have five other depots across England and one in Scotland, none in Wales or Ireland."

Dixon interjected. "An ideal business to be in to poke around without too much suspicion."

Loader nodded. "Exactly, but why the visit by Popov to his house, and what triggered it?"

Bashley said, "A job application?"

Dawn banks didn't think so. "He would go to the office in Basingstoke for that," she said. "He's not likely to visit the MD in his own home, a mansion, miles from where he lives."

"OK, well it's going to be a major job to watch all depots – he's got a total of seventy vehicles running about all over the place. At the moment, we can't justify the cost of a full surveillance, but what I want to do now is to visit Max Turner's place and look around."

DS Gibson's asked, "On what grounds?"

"We'll have to get invited in. Most days Turner and his wife leave home at eight-thirty in the morning and drive to Basingstoke; they normally get back by six o'clock. During the day, there is just a housekeeper and the gardener at the manor house."

DS Gibson asked, "This Max Turner, he's English?"

Loader nodded. "Yes."

"His wife?"

"Don't know yet. We're putting together a fuller biography of them both. Meanwhile, we can only wait and watch until GCHQ come up with the decrypted message."

A Wessex Water van was parked in a lay-by just one mile from Max Turner's manor house. The driver sat in the van relaxing; his mobile rang out.

"Subjects arrived at Basingstoke office," said the disembodied voice.

"OK. Thanks, understood."

The van pulled out of the lay-by, a minute later turned into the gates of the walled estate of the manor house and pulled up at the front door.

The driver, in Wessex Water uniform, got out and rang the doorbell.

It was opened by a smartly dressed woman who glanced at the van, then met Dixon's eyes.

"Hello," she said.

"Sorry to trouble you, Mrs Turner," he said, looking at his clipboard, "but there is a problem with water in the area and we wanted to check if everything is OK here." He smiled, holding up the ID card suspended from a lanyard around his neck.

She laughed. "I'm not Mrs Turner; she is away. I'm the housekeeper, Emily Johnson."

"Oh! Sorry. Anyway, it's just a quick one. There is a break somewhere in the area; we're trying to locate it."

"Well, the water was on at breakfast time."

"That's OK then. Could I ask you to just run the kitchen tap and see if the pressure is OK?"

"Yes of course; I can do that." She turned and led the way inside. Dixon followed her, making a point of loudly closing the front door but then surreptitiously opening it again and leaving it ajar. He followed her into the kitchen. She turned on the kitchen tap. Nothing. A small trickle escaped, then silence.

"Oh dear. It must have gone off in the last hour or two."

Dixon smiled engagingly. Research had been done to check whether Emily Johnson would have more empathy with a male or female visitor. Dixon had been chosen.

"May I just call in?" he asked, taking out his mobile phone.

"Of course," Emily Johnson replied.

Dixon dialled and waited; the call rang out and was answered.

"Hi, Dave here," said Dixon, ensuring Emily Johnson

was listening. "Manor house is out too. Looks like the whole leg is gone. Can you get someone to check the western stop? Let me know ASAP."

He closed the phone, smiled at Emily Johnson. "We're going to check if the whole western leg is out. Is it OK if I wait?"

"No problem. I'll leave you to it." She made to leave.

"Would you mind staying with me, Mrs Johnson? Regulations do not allow us to be in customers' properties alone, in case we nick stuff." He grinned. "It won't take long."

Emily Johnson seemed in no hurry, and Dixon was easy on the eye.

"Oh, all right then. I might as well make a cup of tea while we're waiting. Would you like one?"

"Now you're talking. That's really kind of you but," he held out his arms, "no water!"

She laughed. "There will be enough in the kettle." She busied herself with the cups and teapot.

Dixon turned the tap off and on again as if the act would somehow induce a water flow. He gave a loud, exasperated sigh and sat at the kitchen table.

Silently, the front door was pushed open. Loader, in rubber-soled shoes, padded into the drawing room and on into the library-cum-office. There was a large director's desk in the window bay and a swivel chair behind, two guest chairs in front. One wall was covered with a floor-to-ceiling bookcase. Several steel filing cabinets stood against the other wall, and alongside a large wall map of the UK. There was a further door into an inner room. Loader gently tested it, locked!

He took a photograph of the wall map and riffled quickly through papers on the desk, taking photos as he went. He started to open the desk drawers.

Dixon occupied Emily Johnson in the kitchen. "Do you live here, in the house?" He asked, sipping tea.

"Oh no, I live in Amesbury, come in at nine in the morning till five o'clock. I look after the running of the house. Mrs Turner is away almost full-time."

Dixon continued sipping tea.

"Do they work locally?"

"No, they both go to Basingstoke; they've got a delivery company."

"Oh, d'you mean like DHL?"

"Yes, that's right. It's quite a big company; I'll get you a copy of their brochure."

Before Dixon could say anything, Emily had started to go into the drawing room.

Dickson quickly followed her, calling loudly into the room, "Could you get me a spare copy? I could put one in our office."

"Sure," she said, going into the office.

Warned by Dixon's voice, Loader quickly ducked down on his hands and knees behind the desk.

Emily Johnson glanced about as if she could sense something but went to the filing cabinets and took out a couple of brochures.

Dixon had waited by the kitchen door.

"Thank you, that's helpful," he said, drawing her attention across the room to him as he returned to his seat. She handed the brochures to him, continuing with trivial conversation.

They did not hear the front door quietly open and close.

Dixon's phone rang out.

"Dave," he said. "OK. I'll check." He got up and turned on the tap. A couple of splutters and the water gushed out.

"Eureka," he said into the phone and to Emily Johnson.

"Thank you, Mrs Johnson, all fixed. Thank you for your patience and the tea." He made a note on his clipboard and took his leave.

Dixon returned the van to its owners and went to the Amesbury police station.

Loader and the team were in the incident room. Loader had connected his phone into the media laptop and the copied documents appeared on a wall-mounted monitor.

"Nothing out of the ordinary," he said, scrolling through them. "Mainly schedules and staff matters." He selected the picture of the map. Everyone studied it. There were a number of red spots in various locations, which they took to be where the courier depots were. A larger red dot was stuck over Basingstoke. A couple of routes were highlighted in yellow marker. Nothing else to see.

"Wait a minute!" Banks stood up and approached the screen, looking intently.

"Here, look!" she said to the group.

"Just here, north of Basingstoke, is a sort of discoloration. It looks as if this town was circled with pencil and then rubbed out; there's just a faint mark left."

"Where is it?" asked Gibson from the desk.

Banks reached up and placed her finger on the screen. "Cheltenham."

There was silence, then, in chorus, "GCHQ?"

Loader quickly approached the screen, scanning it intensely.

"Here again!" he said quietly, his finger resting on Norwich. This is too much of a coincidence. They pored over the map more closely – there was a rubbed-out pencil circle around Coningsby and another one at Faslane.

"This is no coincidence!" Loader stated. "It can't be. We need to up the security levels, and we need to visit our friend Turner again."

He was interrupted by his mobile phone ringing out.

"Loader." He listened for a few seconds before standing up abruptly, his face serious.

"OK, I understand. I'll get back to you immediately."

He paced around behind his chair, head bowed in thought, before eventually returning to sit down.

"Ivanov's been located," he said flatly.

Everyone waited. Loader just stared at his notes, unseeing. Then, elbows on the table, he rubbed his hands over his face.

A sudden unthinkable thought was going through his mind.

Dixon broke the silence. "Where has he surfaced?"

Loader pulled himself together. "Norwich!" he said, then went on. "Look, this is too coincidental. I've got to get back to London. I want you to head up this end, Bob. I'm going to put another team together in Norfolk. I'll fill in all the details ASAP. Meanwhile, see what else you can add to Turner's file, find out where all his vehicles travel, do they make bona fide deliveries? Dawn, get yourself to GCHQ and try to push for more info."

Loader collected his file and, as soon as he was alone, called his boss at MI5.

"Hello, Nigel. Can we meet ASAP? Something has come

up, maybe just a straw in the wind, but I need to discuss
with you."

CHAPTER 12

DCI Abbot received a call mid-afternoon. It lasted for thirty minutes and was terminated by the printer in his office downloading two photos and three pages of text. He opened his door into the open-plan office, noting that most of the desks were occupied, officers, male and female, either on telephones or studying computer screens. He caught the eye of DS Reynolds and nodded imperceptibly over his shoulder. By the time he had retrieved the file from the printer and returned to his desk, DS Reynolds had entered his office and quietly closed the door.

"Dick, come in, sit down."

"Sir." Reynolds took the guest chair.

"I've just received a call," the DCI said without preamble. "It seems that we have a priority job on our hands, and I want you to take it up."

"OK, boss."

"Treat this as covert. This comes from the Met, I'm sure at the behest of MI5."

Reynolds was immediately alert. This sort of assignment made a change from the routine cases of theft and traffic. Abbott fiddled with the file on his desk.

"Not much to go on." He handed across the two photos.

"We need to locate these two people of interest. I emphasise maximum discretion. The male is Victor Popov – Russian. Address unknown, whereabouts unknown, last clocked in Birmingham over two years ago. There is no information that he is on our patch. The woman is Greta Adamik, Polish. Address unknown, whereabouts unknown, last clocked four months ago in Solihull. There is a chance that she has moved to Norfolk."

"What are they wanted for?"

"Espionage, I guess, and possible abduction."

CHAPTER 13

The second COBRA meeting was called at short notice at the request of MI5. Prime Minister Grace Armstrong had been advised and would attend. The meeting was held in meeting room 'A'.

Margaret Dibden had driven up from Cheltenham the night before, ready for the early morning start.

As usual, the chief of defence staff, Sir Mark Forsyth, arrived on time, followed shortly afterwards by Frank Gaynor MI6 and the chancellor Keith Brennan. Nigel Phillips MI5 had asked for the meeting; he had arrived an hour earlier.

After opening pleasantries, the PM invited Nigel Phillips to take the chair.

"Thank you, Prime Minister." Phillips quickly gathered his thoughts. "Events have moved forward at an alarming rate over the past few weeks. As you know, after our last meeting, I tasked one of my senior agents, Matt Loader, to investigate the Moscow signal. Matt has been a senior agent in MI5 for a number of years.

"If you are a reader of the *Daily Telegraph*, you already know him as a defence and security correspondent of that paper. He has been engaged in covert work for some time and indeed headed up the original Brown Bear file some five years ago.

"May I, with respect, remind you that his covert activities must remain just that. No breath of what he says must escape from this committee unless formally sanctioned. It's best now that I hand over to Mr Loader – Matt."

Loader was used to speaking to high-level personalities, but he knew that what he was going to say today would stretch his credibility to the utmost. "Thank you, Nigel."

He inclined his head to the prime minister.

"Prime Minister, Brown Bear is, or was five years ago, a covert surveillance operation mounted by Moscow to monitor strategic establishments in the UK. It was disbanded after about twelve months; the ten operatives we identified either left the country or melted into the community. We maintained a watch on them for about a year and then closed the file due to lack of movement and cause.

"We are all agreed that there is little tangible reasoning to call this level of meeting for an activity which is well handled by the security agencies."

He paused, wanting to get his thoughts in order.

"But this reactivation of the programme by Moscow has raised new concerns. We do know, and I've often reported on it, that there is a perceptible increase in security threats to our country, by inference, or even directly, for example excursion into our sovereign sea and airspace. There is increasing cyber intrusion and satellite surveillance. And indeed, Secretary of State," he nodded to Malcolm Bishop, "you have announced major upgrades to our global and strategic aims to contain this.

"The Brown Bear file is an old file that I headed up some five years ago. When I was asked to investigate this reactivation, I assembled two of the agents from my original team. The obvious starting point, until Cheltenham can help us out, was to look up the current whereabouts and activities of those Moscow agents who still remain in the UK. Of the ten Moscow agents, eight have been confirmed as leaving the country. One we have located living in Reading."

He looked across at Grace Armstrong, hesitating.

"Prime Minister, I respect your clinical thinking and your fifth sense in awkward situations, but I hesitate to put the next words to you; you may wish to dismiss them, and me too, but I have spoken at length with Nigel and conclude that what I want to say must be put into the mix."

He drew a deep breath.

"What I am now going to say is absolutely secret, but a story will hit the headlines very soon that will attract world attention; by this meeting you are getting advance notice. In my cover capacity as a defence and security correspondent, I am covering a story that could have unimaginable consequences. I have been working on this for some weeks.

"We can discuss the detail, but in short, I have a contact who is an amateur astronomer, a respected academic. He has built his own radio telescope of a major size which, in addition to receiving signals, also transmits powerful energy into space."

He stopped; there was silence. He went on.

"He has devoted the last twenty years to his project; he is mortgaged up to the hilt. He, and his wife, who is also a

PhD, can no longer cope with the debts. They have agreed to sell their story and findings for a large sum.

"Events have been moving at a fast pace, and in any case, the astronomer, George Newby, knows that at any time soon, NASA or SETI, or some other organisation, will detect the same information and put it in the public domain, thereby depriving Newby of the credit of the discovery and, more importantly for him, reduce the sum that he expects to gain.

"I have negotiated several contracts with publishers for exclusive access to his story and the first parts are ready to be released as we speak."

Loader paused again; he took a drink from his coffee cup. He knew that the next hour was going to make or break him. Although he had tested Newby's thesis to the best of his ability, the very incredulity of the story still made him very nervous. He went on.

"Until two days ago, all this was only of scientific interest, a commercial story. But by a bizarre quirk of fate, I have also been handed the Moscow file, the signal to reactivate the Brown Bear operation picked up by GCHQ. You are aware of the concerns this raised.

"Now, there may be absolutely no connection between these two stories, but here is a scenario in lieu of a tangible connection. Those of you up to date with security matters will know that Russia has launched a series of satellites called the Lotus series. A new Lotus S1 spacecraft was recently launched which manoeuvred a satellite into a circular 560-mile-high orbit to enter service for the Russian military. It is used to gather electronic intelligence and eavesdrop on radio communications.

"In this scenario, say, the Lotus S1 has locked onto the signals transmitted by my astronomer contact and the Russians are deploying agents on the ground to find out more about the signals, and their purpose, and that the increased activity in Sovereign air and sea space intrusion is unconnected."

Loader stopped again. He was again assailed by doubts to the credibility of what he was about say. Too late now!

The defence secretary interjected. "Sounds far-fetched to me!"

The chancellor asked. "So, what are the transmissions about? Do *we* know?"

Loader responded. "I have spent a long time with the astronomer and his wife. I am convinced that they are genuine." He looked at the faces around the table. Senior figures, powerful, knowledgeable, practical.

He squared his shoulders.

"They believe that they are in touch with alien intelligence!"

His announcement was greeted with guffaws and an eruption of voices.

"For Christ's sake."

"You are joking, right?"

"What the hell are you on?"

"This is a serious meeting, Loader!"

"Pull the other one!"

Everyone talked over each other. Loader waited. He noted that only Grace Armstrong remained silent, her eyes on him, quizzical, assessing.

It was the chief of staff who brought order. He slapped his hand flat and hard on the table. The whip-like crack stopped everyone in mid-sentence.

"Enough!" He barked. "This is not a bar room; would you please respect the chair!"

The meeting subsided into silence.

Sir Mark said, "Mr Chairman," deferring to Nigel Phillips.

"Thank you, Sir Mark, colleagues. I anticipated your reaction. I had the same when Loader first told me. I think you have to wait to hear the evidence before judging."

Loader was now in beyond recall.

"Think how the imagination of the world will be captured by this story!" His voice was passionate. "Think back, even before history – man has looked into the black abyss of the night sky and seen the billions of stars suspended in an ethereal mist of cosmic dust and always sought life. Why, even today, billions of dollars have been spent on the latest Mars rover, 'Perseverance', to scrabble around in the Martian dust to look for signs of life.

"More billions are spent by astronomical institutions around the world searching the skies twenty-four seven. At least one major institution, SETI in the USA, is aimed solely at the search for extraterrestrial life. If Newby's discoveries are confirmed, and I believe they will be, then we have a remarkable event in our own backyard."

Loader paused.

"What's SETI?"

"It is an international institution, based in the USA, called Search for Extraterrestrial Intelligence – SETI."

"The man's nuts!"

"That will do, Malcolm!" The PM's voice was calm, authoritative. She looked across at Loader.

"Are the astronomical societies in possession of this remarkable information?"

"No, ma'am."

"Why not?"

"In the field of astrophysics, many discoveries are made by what might be called 'loners' or amateurs. Certainly, my contact is a private astronomer, but after twenty years of research and expenditure, he has reached breaking point. He came to the *Telegraph* office and asked for me by name, knowing that I am a defence and security correspondent; he was hoping I would be able to set up a buyer for his story. He wants to recoup debt and have the discovery attributed to him."

Having restored order, Grace Armstrong looked around the table, inviting questions.

The foreign secretary was first out of the box.

"I'm sorry, but I can't believe that the NASAs of this world have not themselves discovered this and published it."

Loader replied, "Well, they haven't. My contact is sure that this could happen at any time now and is anxious to go public before that happens."

"Where is this contact?" queried the home secretary.

"Newby and his wife have built an observatory in a farmhouse in Norfolk. There are a large number of amateur observatories in the UK and many astronomical societies. The area in Norfolk has been awarded a Dark Sky credential and is a favourite spot for observing the skies."

The defence secretary grumpily butted in. "Let's say this all stands up to scrutiny, what has it got to do with the Moscow covert operation Brown Bear? Which is what we are supposed to be discussing."

Loader replied, "I never linked the two either until

yesterday when I got the news that could be the link to Brown Bear, and my team came up with a scenario."

"Which is?"

"Our first Russian agent, who disappeared off the records in Birmingham years ago, has resurfaced. He has recently moved to Norwich!"

There was silence.

"A weak coincidence!"

"I agree. But last week, the observatory in Norfolk was broken into and ransacked, and we believe Newby, the astronomer, has been abducted!"

"Mr Loader!" Grace Armstrong's voice cut in. "As I understand it, your team are putting forward a scenario wherein Moscow has been alerted to the presence of the Norfolk observatory and that Brown Bear was activated to investigate the nature and purpose of the signals?"

"Yes, Prime Minister. I have coordinated this scenario with the security services, and we agree that the scope of Brown Bear may be limited to this. However, we are alive to the possibility of a darker, more disruptive target. The key will be the results of the GCHQ findings. Meanwhile, we intend to follow up on the Moscow team here in the UK. We do not believe, at this time, that the air/sea incursions are directly linked to Brown Bear, although they may remain a different threat."

The PM now took control of the meeting.

"This is an extraordinary situation! These events are the stuff of science fiction. We must tread very carefully – I strongly suspect a hoax, but we must examine the situation as we find it.

"Mr Loader, as the events – if true – can be construed

to be of national security, I am minded to issue D-notices while we get, as they say, our ducks in a row. Firstly, I want the technicalities of the Norfolk findings to be corroborated by the Royal Astronomical Society. I wish to give our close allies an advance notice of the findings *before* the information becomes public.

"John, please call a meeting of Five Eyes to be held as soon as corroboration is confirmed. Malcolm, please liaise with Helen and the CSA and examine all contingencies.

"Regarding the apparent abduction of Mr Newby. I do not want this placed in the Brown Bear context until we have more information. The matter must be dealt with by the police under missing persons protocol but with added urgency. Communications in these matters will be treated as 'immediate'.

"I expect the RAS to attend the Five Eyes meeting. Following which I will rescind the D-notices and you, Mr Loader, can then release the Norfolk story, without any mention of possible links to Brown Bear or the intercepted Moscow signals."

She paused. "Any questions?"

There was a flurry of queries as the Cabinet members assessed their roles.

Eventually, Grace Armstrong called the meeting to a close. "Very well. We'll proceed at pace. Mr Phillips, it is clear that MI5 and 6 are best placed to coordinate these matters – please issue forward actions and head up the process. The roles of our departments will be clarified following the Five Eyes meeting. I expect all members of today's meeting to be kept fully informed and all communications to be classified Immediate and Top Secret."

The meeting concluded and broke up into animated discussion. Nigel Phillips beckoned to Frank Gaynor, MI6, to join him and Loader.

"We seem to be left holding the baby," he said. Then, looking at Loader, "We'll push this forward as a combined MI5/MI6 file. I propose, since you are at the heart of both the Brown Bear search and the 'green men' story, that you head up a lead team. I will notify all that you have full authority to take control. Agreed, Frank?"

Frank Gaynor nodded, then looked at Loader. "OK by me. I'll get one of mine to contact you later today."

CHAPTER 14

Doctor Jennifer Wright was intrigued to be summoned to the admin offices of Birkbeck, University of London.

Gail, in reception, guided her to a side room where two visitors were seated; they stood as she entered.

"Dr Wright?" smiled Loader, as he offered his hand. "I am Matt Loader." He indicated his companion. "This is Liz Holden."

"Hello," Jennifer Wright replied, with a guarded look. "I have been informed that this is an urgent meeting?"

"Yes, it is." Loader indicated that they sit down. Coffee had been provided. Loader continued. "We represent the Government and security services. I might add that we are approaching you as the current president of the RAS."

Jennifer looked even more puzzled.

"I'm Matt Loader, Senior Agent, MI5. I need to tell you that what we discuss in this room is governed by the Official Secrets Act and I would like to record our conversation if that's OK with you?" He indicated a small recorder that had been placed on the table, then deferred to his companion.

"You may recognise me." Liz Holden smiled, even as recognition dawned on Jennifer's face. "I am Liz Holden, Government Minister and Home Secretary. Is it OK if we use first names?"

Jennifer Wright began to look alarmed.

"Yes of course," she said. "What on earth is this all about?"

Loader diffused the tension by laughing. "Actually, it's not on earth that this is all about. Let us explain."

Jennifer nodded. He went on. "We have a national security situation that needs your help. Besides your role here as a tutor and governor, you are the current president of the RAS; you are also an astronomer and cosmologist. Liz is here to reassure you that we want to discuss a vital matter and that you fully understand it is a genuine request. You may, of course, double-check our identity at any point."

"OK." Jennifer began to relax.

Loader went on. "We have a situation that has immense implications. What we want is corroboration by a recognised authority that the basis is genuine. An amateur astronomer based in Norfolk has made some, er, claims, that we need checking. There are some complications – the astronomer, George Newby, has gone missing—"

Jennifer interrupted him. "George Newby! I know him! He was a professor at Uni of Warwick. Written a number of articles for the journal."

Liz joined in. "Excellent. You knowing who we are talking about will make things a bit easier."

"So, what exactly do you need confirming?"

Loader took up the story. "Newby has a pretty sophisticated radio telescope set up in Norfolk and has been receiving cosmic signals for years now. He is absolutely clear that they are genuinely from extraterrestrial sources."

Jennifer gave a sharp intake of breath.

Loader went on. "We are concerned that the signals could be a hoax or contaminated by terrestrial sources, satellites for example."

Jennifer looked thoughtful. "You could get a second opinion, an expert witness so to speak. But I feel there is more that you are not telling me."

Loader hedged. "There are associated events of a security nature. We intend to inform our allies of the nature of the cosmic signals, if we can be satisfied that they are truly extraterrestrial. So, a direct question, who would be best placed to give us that assurance in a hurry?"

Jennifer grimaced. "In a hurry? I don't think such verification could be done in a hurry; it could take days, weeks, even months to prove."

"We don't have that luxury, Jennifer. I want to get expert witnesses out to Norfolk immediately to look into this."

"Can I ask why the urgency?"

Loader glanced at Liz, who gave an imperceptible nod.

"We believe the signals to be intelligent!"

Jennifer gasped and sat bolt upright.

"You're joking, right?"

"Our first assessment is that it is genuine," Loader said. He omitted to say that the first assessment was his alone.

"Well, it must be a hoax," Jennifer said animatedly. "Do you know how many powerful telescopes are continuously ranged into the skies searching for such an event and have been doing so for years and years? Surely, they would have picked that up by now."

"This is what we want to establish before it gets out of hand."

She looked at Loader grinning at her and coloured.

"I'd say it's a hoax," she said defensively.

The home secretary nodded. "You may well be right. Help us identify an expert who will give an opinion."

Jennifer regained her composure. "I can name two experts immediately who are leading in the field of radio astronomy. Professor Henry Smith, he is a leading astronomer and infrared specialist." She thought for a moment. "Then there's Charles Hewitt, a space scientist and cosmologist. He's always writing about the possibilities of life in the universe. I guess they would soon detect a fraud."

"Excellent," Loader said. "Let's contact both of them and arrange a site visit ASAP. I see from your CV that you, too, are an astronomer and geophysicist – would you join them? Make a team audit."

Jennifer looked enthusiastic.

Loader cautioned her. "Remember. Secret! Nothing must be said at this stage."

CHAPTER 15

Loader checked with the Norfolk Constabulary. There was no news of George Newby.

He called Dixon in Salisbury. GCHQ were no further forward with decoding the Moscow message, and a team were still analysing the movements of Turner's courier vehicles.

He then called Susan. She picked up almost immediately.

"Hi, Susan. How are you coping?"

"Matt!" Susan sounded anxious. "Any news of George? I keep asking the people here, but they don't know anything."

"No, they are only concerned with protecting you, Susan. I have just spoken to the DCI in charge of George's case, but they haven't got anywhere yet. Look, I'm on my way to you now – be there about teatime – is that OK?"

"Of course, Matt, that will be lovely; can you stay?" Her voice sounded tremulous, close to tears. He saw her in his mind's eye and wanted to comfort her.

"I'm staying for a while; there's a lot to talk about, Susan. I've arranged for some people to join us to corroborate George's work; there's a lot more to tell you. Just hang on till

I get there. Everything will be alright – we're together and we'll fix everything."

It was early evening before Loader arrived at the farmhouse. He was tired; it had been a long day.

A security guard waited at the open door, alerted by signal from the main gate. Close behind him stood Susan, who rushed forwards.

"Matt!" She dissolved into his arms.

He held her close for some moments, absorbing her anxiety.

Inside, they stood around the central island in the kitchen, wine glass in hand. The appetising aroma of an evening meal warmed the room.

"Tell me what's going on, what about George?" Susan looked at Loader, her face showing signs of strain.

His voice was gentle. "There's a lot going on behind the scenes," he said. "The county police are carrying out a missing persons protocol; in addition, I've set up a Special Operations team looking at it from another angle."

"What do you mean, *you* have set up a team? What's your role in all this, Matt?"

"There's been a lot of things going on, Susan – I couldn't divulge anything before, but now is the time to share some things with you. I think you've already guessed that I am a bit more than a newspaper correspondent."

"I knew it! Tell me what's going on! Whoever you are, are you the cause of George's disappearance?" There was accusation in her voice that stung Loader.

"No. Of course not; I would never harm you or George. At the time that George first approached me about taking on the story of his research, the radioactivity had already been noticed by foreign interests. At the time, I didn't know what sparked their security system, but it's clear now that they had picked up on George's transmissions, here, from this site. We, that is, our security services, picked up on their interest and we were, and are, investigating it. Besides being a defence and security correspondent for the *Daily Telegraph*, I am a senior agent for the security services. It is purely coincidental that these two strands came together as they did."

Susan still looked miserable. "So, George's work is already common knowledge?"

"No. Not at all. It's the radio transmission signals that have been picked up by the foreign monitors, but they would not have locked onto the received signals and most certainly are unaware of the coded content and their portent. That's why we want to push on with the corroboration and get this story published. That way, we all win. You and George get the recognition, and the money, for the story."

"I wish I knew where George is," Susan said, her voice more conciliatory.

"There's a lot of people working on finding him; please be strong, Susan – it will be OK – we're together, and we'll find him and settle the story too."

After dinner, Loader helped Susan clear away, then they sat in the living room. Susan sat in what was clearly 'her' chair on one side of the fireplace. Loader tactfully sat on a sofa, leaving the second fireside chair unoccupied.

"What's next?" queried Susan as they settled down.

"There is an impossible schedule, Susan; we shall need a lot of input from you, if you are up to it," he added.

"Tomorrow there are three astronomy scientists arriving to take a look at George's work. You'll need to guide them through it – will that be OK?"

Susan smiled ruefully. "I've been working alongside George for almost twenty years now, so I am sure I can point them in the right direction. Some of the technical detail may be beyond me."

"Excellent. As soon as we can get some form of consensus from them, there will be a meeting in London with officials from the Five Eyes; we've already taken a chance and scheduled a meeting for next week!"

"Five Eyes?"

"Yes. It's a group of intelligence and security officials from five countries: Australia, Canada, New Zealand, the United Kingdom and the United States. Basically, a treaty for cooperation in signals intelligence. The PM has insisted that we inform these countries before we publish any whisper of the magnitude of George's work."

Susan looked worried. "I don't think that George anticipated this becoming an international political and security issue."

"Come on, Susan. If this is colloborated it is a world-shaking event! Imagine, intelligent life elsewhere in the cosmos! Scientists for centuries have tried to detect this. It's an unbelievable event, even frightening, and that's before we add in the complication of foreign interference in the radioactivity that George generated! It is a massive global event."

Susan said nothing. Loader could see the strain showing in her face, years of closeted research now exploding into the public domain. He continued gently. "It'll be all right,

Susan; I'll always be here to support you." He reached over and gently held her hand, an expression of feelings he could not admit.

"Let's get the next few weeks done, Susan, then you and George must take a break. A holiday, somewhere warm and simple."

The next day dawned with a flurry of activity.

Dixon phoned in from the incident room in Amesbury. There were no untoward movements in the Turner household, but surveillance of the Turner courier vans was more interesting. While the majority of the fleet went about their business of delivering parcels to addresses throughout the region, Dixon's team noticed that several vans seemed to cruise without any parcel drop-off. They were trying to establish the reason behind it.

The Norfolk Constabulary team investigating Newby's disappearance had no update to offer.

At 8am, two ladies from an outside caterer arrived to provide light lunches, prepare an evening meal and to keep coffee flowing throughout the day. Loader had insisted on this to lighten the load on Susan, who would be key to explaining some of George's work.

At 9am, the police security around the farmhouse changed shifts. Loader was there to thank the outgoing officers and to brief the incoming team: two males, in uniform, and one female, in trousers and floppy jumper.

"There are five visitors arriving this morning," he informed them, "Jenny Wright, Astronomer and Cosmologist, from the Royal Astronomical Society; Professor Henry Smith, Astronomer and Infrared Specialist, from the University of Warwick – he will be bringing along an electronic engineer – Charles Hewittm, Space Scientist and Cosmologist, from the University of London; and finally, Amanda Field, PA to Jenny Wright.

"Please make sure you check their identities on arrival. Any other visitor must be held outside the main gate until you check with me. OK? Thanks. You've got my phone number; stay in touch. The caterers will provide lunch and keep you supplied with coffee."

Shortly afterwards, the visitors began to arrive; introductions were made in the spacious living room. It was a chilly but sunny day; the open French doors led onto the paddock. George's early experimental antenna arrays were visible marching across the field.

Susan appeared tense but easing in conversation with Jenny, who knew of George from earlier astronomical events. Jenny informed her that the party had booked into a hotel in Ely for the night on the assumption that there would still be work to be done the next day.

By 11am, the party was complete. Loader called their attention. "Well, welcome to you all; thank you for responding so promptly. I have to remind you that this is an official brief, governed by the Official Secrets Act. What the Government needs from you is corroboration that the radio telescope you are about to examine is picking up the signals displayed on the oscilloscope monitors, and there is no chance that the signals are from some terrestrial source, either inadvertently or maliciously, or caused by some aberration in the equipment here. Again, please note that what we discuss is subject to the Official Secrets Act until released by the prime minister and security services. Are there any comments before we go on to take a look in the observatory?"

"I'm greatly intrigued," Henry Smith said.

Loader smiled. "OK. Susan has asked me to give you a layman's tour; she will fill in the technical aspects as we go along."

Susan led the way through the hallway and passage to the locked steel door entrance to the observatory.

As the visitors trooped in and stood around the large, central table, they gazed around in astonishment, all talking at once.

Even Loader, used to being in the room, was again assailed by electrostatics.

Loader directed their attention to the door leading to the outside antenna room, everyone following him into the roofless half of the barn, crowding around the large reflector sitting on a scaffolding mount.

"So, the layman's tour," he said. "This reflector is steerable by servomotors from a power generator on the ground floor below us. When you do your assessment, you will see that the antenna is a reflector into a microwave horn feed. The whole assembly produces a pencil-thin field of view. The aerial feed goes directly through the wall here, into a TX/RX splitter in the main room. Let's go back in; you will for sure want to come back out later."

Obediently, they returned to the observatory.

Susan took over the tour, explaining the purpose of the floor-to-ceiling racks of equipment around the room, finally indicating the large blank monitor screen taking up the back wall. "This is where the final signals are displayed," she said, pressing a switch which made the screen come to life, a ragged waveform racing across the screen. "This is the 'white noise effect' that I am sure you are all familiar with. It seems to be accepted that the maximum cosmic reception comes from the constellation of Sagittarius, almost the centre of the Milky Way.

"If you mix it with a stable oscillator, you can 'hear' the radiation. George has done this." She pressed another swich and the room was filled with an ethereal sound, loud, urgent, like a deep-throated frying sound. "Now, we know this is a general mix of radiation from many sources in the sky. What you are seeing, hearing, is the noise from the random spot in the universe where the dish is currently pointing.

"George spent his early years scanning the skies and different wavelengths. He decided that the received energy was too general and designed an antenna with a very focused lobe. The received signals dropped incredibly, but he was able to concentrate on a single point source. He moved the antenna fractionally every twenty-four hours, analysing the signals over a number of wavelengths.

"To cut a long story short, after nearly five years of scanning, he came across a signal that caught his attention. He stopped the scanning, and this is where the antenna is currently focused and has been for over eight years. The result is that, every twenty-four hours, there is a window when the antenna is focused on the source and can track the signal for a few hours."

Henry Smith butted in. "What is the significance of this particular signal?"

Susan switched off the monitor sound. "George knew that signal strength, amplitude, was not a factor and so introduced an amplitude filter, concentrating only on frequency analysis. He had found that this particular source emitted a specific frequency that he could detect on a consistent basis."

She paused, glancing at Loader. He gave an imperceptible shake of his head, then took over the conversation. "You will want to go over this all again and to examine the physical hardware. Tonight, at about eight o'clock, we can convene here again when the actual signals from the source will be lined up. What we need, ladies and gentlemen, is your expert witness opinion that the signals received on this monitor are extraterrestrial and are not contaminated by any terrestrial source. So, Susan and I are here to help you get to grips with the observatory and to assist in any way."

Henry opened the discussion, asking that Bob, the electronics engineer accompanying him, be given a closer look at the circuitry.

"I've spent a number of days with George doing just that," said Loader, "so I can start off, if Susan stands by to correct me." He looked at Susan with a warm smile. "Is that OK?"

She agreed. Everyone wanted to listen in. Loader took them all back into the antenna room and started a physical description from there. He indicated an optical telescope mounted beside the antenna.

"Tonight, we can look through this sighting 'scope, so you can see exactly where we are focused. There is also a camera attached."

Loader then traced the hardware path into the observatory room and the banks of electronics. He outlined the progress of incoming signals to the amplifiers, intermediate amplifiers, the frequency detectors and phase shift detectors, to the final recorders and display circuits.

Susan was able to comment on aspects of the circuitry. As the group's interest grew, the atmosphere became relaxed and animated discussions kept everyone busy until Susan suggested they break for the evening meal.

Drinks were served in the living room while conversations continued, unabated. Loader noted that Susan and Jenny seemed to hit it off and were in light-hearted discussion.

It was nearly 9pm, after a satisfying meal, before the party reconvened in the observatory. By now, the radio telescope was aligned perfectly with the source. Everyone wanted to look through the sighting 'scope. Loader showed them how to take photos of the night sky, which would be printed out for the record.

Back in the observatory, Susan had activated the receivers and recorders.

Amplified cosmic noise waveforms danced across the monitor screens. The sound detectors were also switched on, filling the room with urgent vibrancy. Indicator lights blinked on the banks of racks, indicating their status.

The whole room, now filled with seven people, seemed alive with static and energy.

The night wore on; no one seemed prepared to take a break.

Charles Hewitt, the most seasoned astronomer in the group, was mesmerised.

"I just didn't think we would see a set-up like this. Amazing, George certainly kept this quiet," he said, turning to Susan.

"Well, yes, he has always been a bit of a loner. There's twenty years of his life wrapped up in all this," she said.

Midnight came and went; it was 1am before Jenny, having called the hotel, suggested they call a halt.

"We'd like to come back in the morning," she said. "We'll write up our notes in the morning, examine the equipment some more and spend another evening here, if that's OK?"

"Of course. Same again tomorrow then," Loader agreed, adding, "don't lose sight of why you are here. We want your expert opinion that the signals you are witnessing can be attributed to extraterrestrial origin."

With that, and friendly hugs all round, the tired party left for the hotel.

Alone at last, Loader and Susan sank exhaustedly into armchairs. Susan, who had been animated during the day, describing George's work, now seemed tired and deflated.

Along the hall, in the observatory, cosmic patterns still raced across the screen, recorders capturing the signals for the archives.

Loader looked at Susan's drawn features.

"Tired out?" It was more a statement than a question.

"I wonder where George is," Susan said, her thoughts distant.

"There'll be news soon," Loader tried to reassure her. "There are nearly one hundred officers on the case. Every day, they'll be getting closer to finding him."

His heart went out to her; he could see that the day, standing in for George, had taken its toll. She sat, eyes tearful, unfocused.

He wanted to take her in his arms, to protect and comfort her. Instead, he cajoled her into retiring.

"You need to get some sleep," he said gently. "You did a fantastic job today, Susan, but I'm afraid there's more tomorrow. Come on, now, off to bed. I'm just going to check the security guys and lock up." As they stood, he gave her a brief hug.

"See you in the morning."

The next morning, the visitors were late; it was almost noon before they arrived. Back in the observatory, they had questions.

Bob, the electronics engineer, wanted to look through George's books of circuit diagrams.

The others had gathered around the large whiteboard and were discussing notes and diagrams as they drew on the board.

"An almost unreal situation," said Jenny, who took the lead for the visitors. "We are all astonished by what we see, and although I shall send a written report, we have all agreed that George's astronomy radio telescope is genuine and that the signals captured on the recordings that we have taken can only have come from extraterrestrial sources.

"The most profound and exciting thing is that the detected signals do not have the characteristic form of cosmic noise. As your equipment has shown, there is a defined steady micro frequency that we would hazard to guess could only come from an intelligent source. We are absolutely shocked and cannot wait to follow this up, *but*," she paused, looking around the table, "it does give us a number of issues.

"Firstly, our report will corroborate the fact that the signals detected are extraterrestrial but at this point fall short of attributing them to an intelligent generation. Matt, you have made it clear that these meetings have been conducted within the UK Official Secrets Act, we must respect this, however there are other issues – when authenticated, it will be a global phenomenon; once the genie is out of the bottle, it will be in the public domain and impossible to control. The home secretary has made it clear that the Government intends to share their findings with Five Eyes – yes?"

Loader nodded. "Yes, the meeting is arranged for next week, pending your input. There are some security issues which we need to unravel; once we have shared these issues with Five Eyes, we will remove the story from the Secrets Act."

Jenny went on. "I understand. There are further issues regarding our releasing any information. The UK, in line with eighty-three other countries, is party to a protocol which would require the discoverer, in this case George, to report in a full and open manner to the public, the scientific community and the secretary general of the United Nations. I quote from the Declaration of Principles Concerning the Conduct of the Search for Extra-terrestrial Intelligence:

> "…*If the verification process confirms – by the consensus of the other investigators involved and to a degree of certainty judged by the discoverers to be credible – that a signal or other evidence is due to extra-terrestrial intelligence, the discoverer shall report this conclusion in a full and complete open manner to the public, the scientific community, and the Secretary General of the United Nations. The confirmation report will include the basic data, the process and*

results of the verification efforts, any conclusions and intepretations, and any detected information content of the signal itself. A formal report will also be made to the International Astronomical Union (IAU).

"All data necessary for the confirmation of the detection should be made available to the international scientific community through publications, meetings, conferences, and other appropriate means.

"The discovery should be monitored. Any data bearing on the evidence of extra-terrestrial intelligence should be recorded and stored permanently to the greatest extent feasible and practicable, in a form that will make it available to observers and to the scientific community for further analysis and interpretation.

"If the evidence of detection is in the form of electromagnetic signals, observers should seek international agreement to protect the appropriate frequencies by exercising the extraordinary procedures established within the World Administrative Radio Council of the International Telecommunication Union.

"A Post-Detection Task Group under the auspices of the IAA SETI Permanent Study Group has been established to assist in matters that may arise in the event of a confirmed signal, and to support the scientific and public analysis by offering guidance, interpretation, and discussion of the wider implications of the detection.

"In the case of the confirmed detection of a signal, signatories to this declaration will not respond without first seeking guidance and consent of a *broadly representative international body, such as the United Nations."*

Jenny looked across at Loader and Susan. "The above statements were unanimously adopted by the SETI Permanent Study Group of the International Academy of Astronautics at its annual meeting in Prague, Czech Republic, on 30 September 2010."

CHAPTER 16

Community Police Officer Simmons was on the early shift. Her beat took in parts of the Festival Place and Eastrop Park, Basingstoke.

She liked her job and, over the months, got to know many of the regular shoppers by sight, often extending a cheerful greeting and sometimes a short chat.

Of course, there was sometimes the odd aggressive character, but in the main, Simmons defused each situation with good humour, deflecting excessive abuse.

There was also the occasional drunk, even in the morning, usually overindulgence from the night before.

Sometimes a figure slumped on a park bench was not a 'druggie', nor drunk, but just homeless.

Simmons took everything in her stride. On this morning, she noted one such apparently homeless man slumped on a park bench, eyes forward, unseeing.

As she walked past the man, she guessed him to be about sixty, unshaven and uncombed. He looked as if he lived and slept in his dishevelled herringbone jacket and tan trousers. She went on her way.

Two hours later, her circuit took her past the man again. His position was unchanged. Now slightly concerned, Simmons approached the man.

"Hello, sir, are you alright?"

The man did not acknowledge her question. Simmons donned a pair of gloves from her pocket and gently shook his shoulder.

"Sir, are you OK?" Still no response; he remained slumped. She didn't want to test him for a pulse, pausing indecisively.

A couple walked past without glancing at them. She made up her mind; using her lapel microphone, she called in for assistance.

During the twenty minutes that elapsed before a colleague arrived, there was no movement from the man on the bench.

Simmons' colleague had no such qualms about testing the man's pulse.

"Well, he's alive," he announced, placing a finger on the man's neck. "Best get the medics here."

An hour later, the man was in A&E, Basingstoke and North Hampshire Hospital where, following a series of life sign tests, he was then transferred to an intensive care bed. Later that day, the police were called in to discuss the man's state.

"He's not on drugs, but he has been drugged or poisoned!" the consultant explained. "There is no evidence of recreational drugs in his body. But he is very ill. There are traces of variants of sodium thiopental in his body and some other elements. His lack of reaction to nerve stimulus suggests some form of poisoning."

The detective sergeant took notes.

"Any ID on his clothes?"

"No. His clothes are in a sterile bin for now. It's a waiting game; we're just trying to keep him alive until the body recovers or we find an antidote."

"Right, I'll get Missing Persons on it. I'll take photos of his clothes for the file."

The consultant nodded. "OK, I'll take you along."

CHAPTER 17

The COBRA briefing room was rapidly filling, even over an hour before the scheduled start of the meeting.

Early arrivals stood around in groups; there was a buzz of muted expectancy.

The agenda had been deliberately vague, an innuendo of global importance, a mixture of political and security attendees fuelling speculation.

Loader and Susan had arrived even earlier to set up the audiovisual system, preparing a PowerPoint presentation to follow the day's agenda.

The briefing venue had been changed to accommodate over forty participants around a central table; further chairs were arranged along the walls behind the delegates for the use of aides.

Unusually, the prime minister, Grace Armstrong, was also early, meeting and greeting the ambassadors and security chiefs from each of the four nations of the Five Eyes protocol.

The home secretary, foreign secretary, defence secretary, MI5, MI6, GCHQ and chief of staff represented the hosts.

Grace Armstrong, elegant as ever, thought Loader.

"Are you all set to make your presentation and to field questions?" she asked.

"Yes, Prime Minister. Susan Newby is here, and Jenny from the RAS is on hand to cover technical questions, so we are all set."

"Good." The PM moved on; Loader noted that she stopped for some time talking to Susan; the two seemed in earnest conversation and, despite her early misgivings, Susan looked confident and engaged.

Promptly at 9am, a personal assistant called the room to order. Everyone took their places and stood until the PM, who was having a last word with her PA, moved to the head of the table. "Ladies and gentlemen. Thank you, please be seated." She sat down and surveyed the room as the shuffling of chairs died away and forty faces looked at her expectantly. Introductions were quickly made.

"Thank you all for attending this briefing, I agree, at very short notice. I'm sure you've speculated on the agenda items and I'm also sure you will leave this room today stunned by the enormity of what we discuss. So, I'll waste no more time.

"We have a situation, a security issue which we were, and are, handling domestically. What we have learned through amazing coincidence is that the issue is linked to an astonishing discovery made by a British astronomer George Newby. It is difficult to comprehend what is going on, and in the middle of everything, George Newby has himself disappeared, we fear abducted!"

A collective intake of breath caused Grace Armstrong to pause. There followed utter silence, the audience mesmerised, waiting for more detail.

She continued. "Our thoughts are with George's wife Susan, who is with us today and is the key link to some extraordinary events. Susan will support MI5 in their presentation today."

Grace Armstrong smiled fleetingly across the room to Susan, a subtle signal of support. She went on. "Why this meeting? What you are going to hear will have global repercussions. I am anxious that you, close friends and our allies, through your intelligence authorities, can report back to your countries immediately. I want you all to be ahead of a general release into the public domain, which will be next week.

"So now I propose to ask our intelligence service MI5 to brief us all. A transcript will be released to you at the end of the meeting. Mr Loader."

Loader stood. He preferred to stand when delivering a talk, as distinct from a discussion.

"Thank you, Prime Minister. As this is the first most of you will have learned about this situation, I propose to start at the beginning. These events began with an encrypted signal detected by GCHQ which activated a covert Russian group here in England, code-named Brown Bear.

"Although we have not yet been able to decode the content, we deduced that the aim of Brown bear is to identify the source and intent of electronic activity emanating from a specific area of this country. We have also deduced that the radio energy has been detected by the Russian satellite RS.

"However, the background to our investigations is further complicated by the expansion of Russian aims in Ukraine and ever more intrusion into sovereign airspace. While all this has been occupying our intelligence services, and by astonishing coincidence, I was approached by George Newby to buy his story, a story of pure science fiction as I first thought.

"In the course of due diligence, I got to know George and his wife Susan very well. Susan is with us today." He glanced at her sitting next to him. She smiled self-deprecatingly and nodded.

Loader continued. "George is a radio astronomer of unequalled technical expertise; he has pursued his private quest for over twenty years with Susan by his side. He started out with cheap government surplus hardware, bought a farmhouse in Norfolk and built his first radio telescope. Since then, he and Susan have devoted all their earnings to building ever more sophisticated equipment."

He paused, this time for a long period. There was silence in the room.

"Well, nine years ago, George detected a signal he believed – knew! – could only be from an intelligent source."

There was a collective intake of breath, everyone in the room sitting upright.

"He spent a further year devising verification circuits and developing a transmitter to work alongside the receiver telescope. Eight years ago, he switched on his transmitter in response to the received signals. And then nothing! The received signals continued from the same source; George's transmitter continued to send out the same response. And so, it went on, twenty-four seven, month after month, year after year."

He paused dramatically.

"Two months ago, George's radio telescope picked up a change to the sequence, *a new sequence that recognised his transmissions of eight years ago!* George is totally convinced the signals are genuine. Since then, we have had the privilege of having the UK RAS corroborate the signals. Susan has collaborated George's work but has an even more startling hypothesis."

Loader stopped. The enormity of what he was trying to explain to the world statesmen gathered here sank in. He looked at the girl by his side, attractive, composed.

"Susan?" he said, seeking support. She looked momentarily startled.

"Oh! Well, yes. George was beside himself with the technical side of the received signals. I am more taken with the significance of my own interpretation, which takes events a step further." She glanced at Loader; he nodded; she drew a breath.

"My interpretation is that not only do the signals confirm extraterrestrial intelligence *but also that whatever intelligence generated them is on its way here!*"

The delegates could keep silent no longer, bursting into a cacophony of interruptions.

Loader held up his hands, palms out. "Ladies and gentlemen! Please wait. I will go over the timeline with you and then we can answer questions." The noise subsided.

Loader turned to the large screen and the presentation. The first pictures were of the farmhouse in Norfolk, the observatory with the banks of equipment and then the antenna mounted in the outer barn. Loader described the barn and its technical equipment, then brought up a picture of the waveform, first a horizontal line of noise.

"This is where the information is," he said. "If I expand the axis, you will see the steady waveform becoming clear.

It is this frequency that the radio telescope is receiving. What George discovered through his signal-processing equipment were unexplained phase shifts, unexplained, that is, until he examined a longer period. And then he discovered an awesome characteristic."

By now, the room of forty people were transfixed. Silent.

Loader continued. "George made idealistic diagrams for me. He drew a vertical red line every time there was a phase shift; you can see it on this slide." Loader moved to the next slide which showed several vertical red lines spaced along the waveform. "Each vertical line represents a phase shift occurring in the signal. The next slide shows the effect over a longer time."

The next slide appeared. "Look, starting at the left. One vertical red line, then a gap, then two red lines close together, a gap, then three red lines, a gap, then four red lines, a longer gap, then the sequence starts over again. Do you see? A basic one, two, three, four series repeating itself indefinitely. These were the signals that George analysed some nine years ago."

He paused for questions. This time there was not a rush of voices; people were absorbing what Loader had shown.

He went on. "OK. As soon as George got over the shock of his discovery, and after some time proving to himself that the signals were not some terrestrial hoax, he built a transmitter that mimicked the frequency and its phase modulation. He then moved the frequency marginally and beamed a code back towards the alien source; that code was again a mathematical progression, this time two, four, eight, sixteen.

"For eight years, there was no further movement; the signals continued to be received and to be sent. Then, two months ago, George's alert system detected a change to the pattern. The received signals now showed a repeat of what George had sent but with an astonishing difference. Please look at this slide."

All eyes stared at the presentation; George had simply written a line of figures across the screen. Two, four – thirty – eight, sixteen.

The assembly stared at the screen for some seconds then a more mathematically minded voice shouted, "Oh my god! I see it! Thirty is the sum of the progression!"

Loader held out his hands. "Yes, it is. This is absolute proof that these extra-terrestrial signals are carrying intelligence."

The dam of questions burst, everyone speaking at once.

The Australian security representative's loud voice rose above the cacophony of the rest. "This can't be! It's got to be a cyber scam. Somebody's having a joke on you!"

"Why?" said another.

"It's all too simple," replied the Australian. "Counting one, two, three, four? If there was something out there, it would be a bit more sophisticated."

"Not so," chipped in the US security representative. "All they are doing is seeking a response. They're hardly likely to converse in English!"

"What does NASA say?"

"Have you even told NASA?"

Loader quelled the outburst with raised hands.

"*Wait*! Wait. What you have learned so far can be supported by scientific fact. Think about it." He counted off on his fingers. "One. The radio energy to the best of all tests is extra-terrestrial. This has been agreed by the three astronomers from the British RAS. Two. George Newby himself is a respected PhD in the field of astrophysics; Susan too, is well qualified in the field. Three. What would we expect any extra-terrestrial energy to look like? As one of us said here, we're hardly likely to receive a 'good morning, Earthlings'…"

There was a smattering of laughter.

Loader continued. "Four. What we are sharing with you is brand-new but is about to go into the public domain for full scrutiny."

Animated conversation broke out again, forty voices trying to understand what they were hearing.

"Colleagues!" The Prime Minister's crystal voice cut through the buzz. "May I remind you that, as Mr Loader has said, this is all but weeks old. Soon, every radio telescope on the planet will be focused on this source. My intention is to inform you all here in advance of the release of data. Do not forget there is a security issue mixed up in all this. Your authorities need to study the briefing carefully; it may be more complex than appears at first sight."

Grace Armstrong paused. "This government intends to release the observatory part of this discussion to the public domain next week, and on Tuesday, Mr Loader will be the author of a four-page spread in the *Daily Telegraph*. I understand it is also being released by the *Daily Telegraph* group to a number of other papers and magazines. From then on, it's up to the public to make of it what they will. You will have full disclosure documents at the end of this meeting and must get them immediately to your administrations. If it is indeed a hoax, it will soon be uncovered and soon forgotten but, ladies and gentlemen, suppose it is real? What then?"

There was utter silence as the full significance sunk in.

She continued. "Imagine the event! The most far-reaching story in the history of humanity. How long have we searched for life outside our world? The ramifications will be unparalleled. If intelligent, what does this extra-terrestrial energy mean? Is it a threat to our world or not? For this reason, my government is laying out every detail of what we know to you, our friends and allies. As for the implications, we have called for a meeting of the United Nations, as required by the protocol, to discuss a global position.

"At the same time, we are releasing the data to all national observatories on request and specifically to our RAS, to NASA and to SETI. Please feel free to continue questions to our team here."

Grace Armstrong looked around the table; there were more questions, lots of them.

The Canadian ambassador, who had been quiet during the discussion, raised his hand. "Mr Loader, this is a question for Mrs Newby, really. It is suggested that the radio signals indicate aliens may be on their way here?" He paused to receive a nod of affirmation. "This is a bold assumption if I might say so. Can you expand on this?"

Loader nodded. "Yes. The radio telescope signals are a matter of technical fact, including the embedded intelligence. Mrs Newby, Susan, has a hypothesis that the signals embody a message. I might add that Susan is a cognitive psychologist and has written several papers on the subject."

He turned to Susan. "Susan, would you take this one?"

She smiled, slightly on edge.

"Well, yes. I agree that my reasoning will be scrutinised around the world, raise some eyebrows and different opinions will be aired. The content of the received signals is a fact. The conclusion is my own. I have based this on my work in neuroscience and in seeking the 'how' and 'why' of the human condition. Clearly, aliens – with no concept of human communication – will not address us in our own language, for example, 'we are coming to tea.'"

There was a murmur of mirth.

She went on. "So, any first contact must be based on some formula which is cosmic in reach; this has to be maths. Now, while what we have is not mathematical in the sense that it solves or proves a theorem, it does follow a general agreement that a lot of development is achieved by association. By generating the sum of the sequence, i.e. thirty, the intelligence is confirmed. By placing the number within our own progression, I believe the originators associate themselves within 'our' intelligence.

"One can interpret this to mean something or nothing. My own view is that the originator of the number thirty intends to be within our society. That is, to visit us. I can only leave it to the others to make their own conclusions."

There was silence as the assembly absorbed her words.

Grace Armstrong suggested that the meeting break for refreshment and informal discussion and be reconvened in an hour for final briefing.

Delegates stood around to stretch their legs; coffee was served. The room filled with a buzz of conversation as everyone discussed the implication of what they had learned.

Loader, talking to Nigel Phillips about the latest information on Newby's abduction, noted that Susan was surrounded by several delegates and engaged in animated conversation.

After fifty minutes, the meeting reconvened until all aspects of the situation had been explored.

The prime minister closed the meeting. "Thank you all for attending. A full brief is ready for you to take away. Please ensure that you report back to your administrations without delay. Finally, I remind you that the information will be in the public domain next week."

Loader and Susan took a taxi to his apartment in Chelsea; it was the end of a tiring day, and they agreed it would be best if Susan stayed at his apartment and then they would both travel to Norfolk the next morning.

They relaxed into armchairs, looking out through the floor-to-ceiling windows overlooking the Thames.

"Wine?" Loader asked.

"Please." Susan gave a tired smile and stared out of the window, watching a passenger ferry bustle downstream.

"Where do they go?" she asked.

"That one is probably heading to Greenwich."

She sighed. "So much has happened since George decided to open up. Do you know, I haven't been to London for years, well," she added, "I haven't been anywhere for years."

They sat in companionable peace, wine glasses in hand.

"I wonder where George is," Susan pondered aloud. "He should be here doing all this. It's been his life for twenty years, and now all people are going to know about him is that he's missing."

"We'll find him," Loader said gently. "There are a lot of people searching."

"I hope he is alright."

Loader reached out and wrapped her hand in his. "We're doing all we can, Susan. Meanwhile, we'll look after his work until he returns."

Susan looked tired and suddenly vulnerable. Loader wanted to take her in his arms, protect her.

"I tell you what," he said, "you go and have a relaxing bath; I'll order a takeaway, and then we'll plan tomorrow."

The next morning, they drove to the farmhouse. Loader had alerted both security and the housekeeper that they were on their way.

On their arrival, they found that the kitchen had been stocked and the house warm. Loader saw that Susan, who had been nervous about returning, visibly relax.

After lunch, they opened up the observatory. The power was still on, the many indicator lights glowing. Susan did a quick check that the system was operating, switching on the monitor recordings, reassured by the familiar waveform across the screen. She expanded the timescale.

"This was last night," she explained, studying the phase shift markers. "Nothing's changed."

They spent an hour mooching around the room, looking out at the radio telescope mount, checking that all was well. The room was warm and felt comforting, a soft hum of transformers lending atmosphere.

Back in the living room, Loader said he would need to return to London the next morning. There was still formatting, and editing, required to the four-page article he had prepared, which was due to be published next week.

There was also liaison to be done regarding associated publication releases.

"I shall be picking up a sizable cheque for you next week. And once the story is released, you will be inundated with media interest." He looked across at Susan. The disappointment that he was leaving was clear in her eyes.

CHAPTER 18

Loader was in the *Daily Telegraph* offices when the call came.

"Matt, this is Bob Dixon. We've located Newby!"

Loader's attention immediately switched from the copy he had been studying.

"Where is he? How is he?"

"Not good, Matt. He's in the Basingstoke and North Hampshire Hospital. He's in some sort of coma. Local police found him in the park. I've put a security cordon around everything and his room."

"Good work, Bob, where are you now?"

"Still in Amesbury. I've called the area centre terrorism unit to get here and take it up."

"Right. Can we set up a meeting tomorrow morning? Then we'll visit Newby after."

"Can do. Not much point in visiting Newby though. I understand he's not responding."

"OK. But we'll both go up there and see what the background is."

"OK. See you in the morning." Dixon hung up.

Loader was torn about telling Susan. He didn't want to tell her over the phone but couldn't get to Norfolk. In the end, it had to be a phone call. He made it as gentle as possible. Susan's reaction was a mixture of fear and relief.

"Is he alright, Matt?" she asked tearfully.

Loader hedged. "He's under sedation; we'll find out more tomorrow. But he's safe, Susan, and in good hands. I've arranged a car to pick you up tomorrow at midday and take you to Basingstoke. They've set aside a room for us to meet before you go in. Julie will come with you. Stay with her until I get there."

Her voice was tremulous. "OK, Matt."

Loader's mind was a chaos of emotions. Only three days to go before the global release of information about extraterrestrial intelligence. An earth-shattering and international story in itself.

On top of this was the hunt for the covert operation Brown Bear. From what Bob Dixon had said, it looked as if Newby had been drugged or poisoned.

The possibility that Newby had been poisoned took on serious connotations.

Was it linked to Brown bear? Was the whole choreography of Russian incursions and the current operation linked?

He was now deeply involved with George and Susan Newby and their quest to finance debts. On top of everything, he was attracted to George's wife. His reverie was cut short by another incoming call. It was Margaret Dibden. GCHQ.

"Hello, Matt. We've cracked the Brown Bear code! As we suspected, it activates a surveillance brief, little more.

One part that concerns us is that it mentions 'phase one'. I'll come to London and discuss."

"Margaret, I'm totally overwhelmed at the moment – George Newby has been found! He seems to have been drugged. Anyway, he's in a coma in the Basingstoke and North Hampshire Hospital. Is there any chance we could meet up there tomorrow afternoon? I've got a meeting room organised. Susan Newby will be there and CTU."

"Yes. I can do that," Margaret said. "I'll see you there then, timing?"

"Say three o'clock?"

Loader spent the rest of the day finalising the draft of the four-page article that would appear in the *Daily Telegraph* next Tuesday, the date agreed by Government for release.

The headline, spread across the pages, was stark: 'Alien intelligence discovered'.

There was a picture of the night sky, constellations marked out. An arrow pointing to the area of the source of received energy.

The spread included head-and-shoulder pictures of Susan and George Newby, a dissertation of their academic status and their self-imposed twenty-year search for life in the cosmos.

There was a picture of the farmhouse observatory and antenna mount, but the central pictures were of the monitors, showing recordings of the processed signals buried in the cosmic noise, the final picture showing the superimposed phase shift markers.

The text examined the import of the discovery, its possible impact on life on earth.

Loader had reported on the Five Eyes meeting and the calling notice for a UN gathering the next week.

The next morning, Loader drove to Amesbury. The team were already there when he arrived. The counter terrorism officer had joined the group.

"Righto. Let's summarise what we've got. I've got to be away by one o'clock to visit Newby."

Loader briefed the team on the bigger picture. Then Dixon updated everyone on the discovery of Newby, his transfer to the hospital and initial prognosis. Regarding the surveillance of Max Turner, there was no new information.

"I do have some news though!" Dixon said. "Norfolk Constabulary located Greta Adamik yesterday and will interview her today, and we'll hopefully get Ivanov!"

The CTU officer, John Finlay, spoke up. "I've followed the brief on the surveillance; if Newby has in fact been drugged or poisoned by Russian agents, we are in a new ball game. Who carried it out, how was it done? It means that there are characters out there willing to conduct overt terrorism. It becomes a hostile act on sovereign territory; the stakes will be higher; and the threat level will go up."

Loader agreed. "You're right. Once we find out what has happened to Newby, we'll take a direct approach to Turner and Co. but for now, we'll see how Newby plays out."

The team discussed the surveillance operation, noting that the distinctive vans of Turner's couriers seemed to be on a legitimate business, but still five vans had seemed to take aimless journeys. The Wiltshire Police member noted that the journeys occurred in the areas of security interest.

"Carry on tabbing them," said Loader. "A few 'stop and search' sound in order. We might also pay another visit to Turner's mansion. We'll decide tomorrow on the next steps."

The meeting broke up at 12.30pm and Loader was on the road to Basingstoke hospital by 1pm.

As he came out of the car park, walking to the main reception, Susan was getting out of the official car, driven by Julie. He called her name and hurried towards her, enveloping her in a close embrace.

"Matt!" she cried, worry and tiredness etched in her face.

"Shh," he whispered in her ear. "I'm here now. We're together. Let's go in and see how George is."

They went into reception, Susan holding onto Matt's arm for support and comfort. They were expected and smoothly ushered to a side room.

Dixon, Finley and Margaret Dibden were already there. There was a coffee jug and cups on a side table.

"I will tell the consultant that you're here," said the receptionist.

Loader introduced Susan to Finley. He didn't expand on the terrorism role that Finley had mentioned.

Dixon and Dibden, Susan already knew; she sat, cradling her coffee cup in both hands. Loader could see that events were taking their toll. He held back an overwhelming desire to hold her in his arms, to comfort her. Instead, he gently placed his hand on her shoulder, willing his strength, through contact, to infuse her.

After a few minutes, the receptionist returned, accompanied by a man carrying a file in his hand. He stepped forward.

"John Goodyear. Consultant Toxicologist," he said, addressing Loader who had stood up to meet him. Loader introduced him to the group.

"Ah, Mrs Newby," he said, addressing her gently.

"Can I see George?" she asked.

"Well, yes. I'm afraid he is still sedated but why don't you go on with Nurse Blake here, and we'll catch you up."

Susan put down her cup and stood up to go, giving Loader a fleeting appeal.

"We'll join you very shortly." Loader's heart ached.

With Susan gone, the consultant sat with the others, opening his file.

"Is he totally unable to talk?" asked Finley.

"He cannot communicate in any way. And is seriously unwell. We have placed him in a protective coma while we try to purify his blood. We have also pumped his stomach to remove any residue that may remain. We need time."

Loader gave a loud sigh. "Prognosis?"

"Too early to say. There were traces of sodium thiopental in his blood. It could be that an overdose was administered."

"Sodium thiopental?" asked Finley.

"We think he had a truth drug administered and that the perpetrator got carried away." He went on. "It would be useful to know the context in which Newby found himself a target and who might be responsible."

Loader explained. "Newby is an academic and an astrophysicist. He has discovered some exciting things through radio astronomy. It will be in all the newspapers next week. We think his activity triggered some form of alarm in the Russian cyber monitoring system and that a covert Russian operation here in the UK have tried to extract information from him, not realising that all of Newby's work will be public knowledge anyway in a few days' time."

"I see. Certainly, the Russians have form in this country. I'm thinking of the poisoning in Salisbury some time ago. I will double-check, but I don't think Newby has suffered any form of nerve agent poisoning. It wasn't intended to kill, more like trying to get him to talk."

"That's daft! He would have talked anyway, without inducement."

"Yes. Maybe he did, but perhaps they didn't believe him and were trying to force a non-existent story from him."

Margaret Dibden spoke up. "I believe that the abductors could be the Russian covert team. I've got here the Brown Bear message that was transmitted – we finally got it decoded." She took a file from her briefcase. "The first paragraphs are activation orders, instructions to monitor any increase or unusual activity around sensitive sites. There is then a list; it includes your department and GCHQ, several military sites around the country, especially naval and submarine bases. The orders are to monitor and report. But then there is a specific order to locate and explain the source of unusual electronic activity in the Norfolk region.

"I think the activity had been picked up by their new satellite. We have picked up several messages sent back to Moscow from a number of locations around the country. I'll hand you the file, Matt. Anyway, we believe that the Brown Bear group were responsible for the responses to Moscow."

"You're probably right. We still do not have enough data to go after a number of people who may be involved."

Loader turned to the consultant. "I think you can see the link between events and the situation with Mr Newby. Please remember this conversation is subject to the Official Secrets Act for the moment."

"Of course. Well, shall we join Newby and his wife?"

They trooped off along several corridors. There was a uniformed police officer outside Newby's room.

Loader led the way in. Susan was sitting at the bedside, holding George's hand. Her face was bleak. Newby was wired up and assisted by oxygen. He had been shaved and his hair combed, but Loader was alarmed by his appearance. He had lost weight and looked considerably older. He stood by Susan's shoulder while Dixon and Finley and the consultant stood around the bed.

There was nothing really to say and soon the group broke up. Loader told Dixon that he did not want to start any operations until Ivanov had been flushed out. Meanwhile, the team should keep up with the surveillance.

There was just Loader and Susan left in the room with George. Susan looked up at Loader, still standing, her face tearful. Lost.

"I don't know what to do, Matt."

Loader's gut wrenched. "He's in good hands, Susan, you must let the experts take care of George. Honestly, there is nothing you can do until he comes round."

"Do you think he can hear me?"

"I don't think so; he's in an induced coma to help him get better. There's little you can do except stay strong and look after his interests."

They sat for a long time; Loader spoke quietly. "I think the best thing you can do, Susan, is to go back home and wait for news. You will be told as soon as there is any sign of consciousness; then you can come back."

She nodded miserably.

"Look I'll go and bring the car to the front; you can come out when you feel ready."

There was no response. Loader gave Susan a gentle squeeze on the shoulder and quietly left the room.

He had been sitting in the car for almost an hour before Susan came out of the hospital. They drove back to Norfolk mainly in silence. Susan wrapped in misery and uncertainty.

Loader, too, was silent, his mind trying to juggle the international situation about to unfold, the hunt for the Russian agents and his love for Susan all vying for attention.

Yes! For the first time, he was prepared to openly admit that he was in love with Susan, an impossible situation and unrequited. Susan leant on him desperately for support and guidance but had never given him cause to hope his feelings were reciprocated.

They arrived at the farmhouse late in the evening. Susan just wanted to retire. She gave Matt a hug.

"Thank you for all that you're doing, Matt. I'd be lost without you."

Loader held her close for a moment, his heart aching.

Next morning, Loader was up early. He was already on the phone with Dixon and the police teams. There was no change in George's condition.

He discussed the options of picking up Turner and Popov for questioning, but they decided it would have to wait until Ivanov was found.

Nigel Phillips, MI5, called. There was to be yet another emergency COBRA meeting. The PM wanted the Government to have clear contingency plans for every conceivable event in the wake of the media release due out next week.

Loader groaned. "Nigel, I'm over my head here with Newby's hospitalisation and Brown Bear. I'd rather stay here and handle this end for the time being."

Phillips agreed that he would represent MI5 at the meeting.

Jan from the *Daily Telegraph* office called. "Hi, Matt. Just thought you'd like to know we've now syndicated your story to over a hundred papers and magazines across the globe. The copy will be released eighteen hours before publication. We've drafted in every available journalist to follow up over the next few weeks. Everyone here knows something big is afoot; it's hard to keep a lid on it until Tuesday!"

"You must, Jan! You're sure everything has been done on a need-to-know basis?"

"Yep. The copy is finalised and in the safe until Monday."

Loader was restless, the situation closing in all around him. It was Thursday, just four days to go before the world-shattering events were relayed to the world.

There was already a discernible layer of tension throughout the global media; everyone knew something was about to happen but did not know what.

He made a cafetière of coffee and took it into the observatory. This one place seemed comforting, a quiet murmur of electronic devices. He switched on the monitor screen and, for a while, stared unseeingly at the recorded noise signals.

Idly, he moved the scale, as George had instructed him, expanding the axis until he could discern the processed underlying waveform. Everything looked the same. The room was warm, the air filled with an energy that only accentuated the feeling of security.

He riffled through the files laying on the table, the content that had provided the rationale behind the information about to be released to the world.

Susan came into the room still in her dressing gown. She looked pale but composed.

"I thought I'd find you here," she said.

He poured her a coffee. "Good morning, Susan. I just felt more settled in here."

"I know what you mean. Even after years of time spent in this room, I feel happy here."

"The next few days, even weeks, are going to be hellish, Susan. Everything is happening at once, and I'm rushing around like a mad thing, but I shall always be around to support you."

"I know," she said simply.

CHAPTER 19

DS Reynolds, Norfolk Constabulary, took the files of Victor Ivanov and Greta Adamik back to his desk and ran the names through the usual databases.

Ivanov drew a blank, but Greta Adamik was easy – her driving licence came up, legitimate. The DVLA database provided a current address, an unpretentious semi-detached house in the outskirts of Norwich.

Reynolds ordered an immediate discreet surveillance of the property. An inconspicuous family saloon arrived at the end of the street, two occupants, plain-clothes police officers. The following evening, Reynolds visited.

He tapped on the driver's window.

"Hi, Tom, how are you doing?"

"Boring, guv. Female left at eight o'clock this morning, got back at five-thirty. No other traffic. She's the one in the photo alright."

"Good. OK. Have a look round the back while I have a chat."

They moved down the street to Greta Adamik's house. Reynolds rang the bell. The door was opened cautiously.

From the photo records, it was clearly Greta Adamik, but formalities were needed.

"Greta Adamik?" asked Reynolds.

"Yes," the woman said guardedly.

Reynolds held up his warrant card.

"DS Reynolds, Miss Adamik. I'm hoping you can help us with our enquires?" The woman looked fleetingly anxious, then pulled herself together.

"How can I help you?" she asked, making no move to let Reynolds in.

"I'm looking for the whereabouts of Victor Ivanov. We believe he is a friend of yours. Er, could I come in and discuss it?"

Adamik was clearly reluctant to admit Reynolds. She gave a fleeting glance back into the house, before standing aside. Her body language told Reynolds that someone else was in the house; he said nothing as they entered the living room.

"You do know Victor Ivanov?" began Reynolds as there was a sudden commotion outside the back door. Reynolds ignored Adamik and strode into the kitchen, opening the back door.

A man lay on the back lawn, the surveillance officer kneeling on his back.

"You were going somewhere?" said Reynolds conversationally, adding. "I think we've got enough to book you for assaulting a police officer, don't you think, Tom? Get him down to the station." He waited until the man was handcuffed and led round the house to the surveillance car.

"I take it that was Ivanov?" Reynolds said to Adamik. She nodded dejectedly.

"Why are you doing this?" she asked. "What's Victor done?"

"Assaulted a police officer for one thing," said Reynolds. "We're just going to have a chat with him at the station, could have done it here if he hadn't tried to do a runner."

He took his leave and called into DCI Abbott.

"Suspect on way in, gov."

Abbott called Dixon, MI5, who called Loader. "We've got Ivanov!"

SATURDAY MORNING

Traffic was running smoothly southbound on the A3 towards Portsmouth, that is, until half a mile before a lay-by, a police car in the flow of traffic switched on its 'blues and twos' and began a rolling roadblock, slowing the traffic. At the lay-by, waiting traffic police stepped out, selecting several vehicles and waving them into the lay-by. One was a yellow Transit van bearing the logo: 'Turners Express Couriers'.

On the pretext of impartiality, two vehicles were cursorily examined, but the target was the yellow Transit van.

The driver looked enquiringly through his open window at the police officers.

"We're doing a traffic survey, sir, won't take long," the officer said in a friendly voice. "We just like to ask a few questions."

"What do you want to know?" The driver spoke in an Eastern European accent.

"Driving licence?"

A man fished in his pockets, producing a photo ID. The second police officer walked around the van, examining the tyres.

"Thank you, Mr Polsky, where are we heading today?"

The man took his licence back. "Got a drop-off in Portsmouth and Southsea."

"Parcels and stuff?" queried the officer conversationally.

"Yeah. Picked up from our depot in Basingstoke."

"Could we take a quick look in the back?" The officer's tone remained friendly. The man shrugged, got out of the vehicle, walked to the back and opened the rear doors.

There was very little in the van, about ten large cardboard boxes of assorted sizes and a chair.

The officer took a cursory glance at the parcels.

"What's the chair for?" he asked.

The driver shrugged. "Sometimes I sit outside with a coffee or sandwich."

The officer noted that the floor of the van seemed to have excessive abrasive marks near the cab. He climbed into the back, eyeing up the rear of the cab. He rapped his knuckles on the wall.

"Seems odd," he said. "This doesn't seem to be the back of the cab."

The driver shrugged; it seemed to be his mode of communication.

"I think this is a false panel!" said the officer after further inspection. He went on, "I reckon this opens up."

The driver gave his now universal shrug.

"OK. Open it up!" The officer's tone took on an edge.

The driver glanced around, as if weighing up his options, then got into the cab and inserted a rod into a small hole in the back panel, which released the door to a large compartment, revealing a cabinet of electronic equipment.

All three stared at the equipment in silence for some moments.

"Well, well! What have we got here then?"

"Sat nav," said the driver. "We get sent to some very difficult addresses sometimes."

The officer reached into his pocket and pulled out a mobile phone, thrusting it towards the driver's face.

"This, sunshine, is sat nav! All that kit there," he indicated the bank of electronic equipment, "is not! You're coming to the station with us. The van will be moved on a low loader for examination."

"On what charge?" the driver demanded, showing some signs of agitation.

"Murky behaviour! Just get in the car!"

The following day, Loader received a call from Dixon.

"Boss, we've got a Turner van. Picked it up on the A3. Forensics have just reported in. It's serious."

"Go on!"

"OK, it's stuffed full of eavesdropping electronics, hidden in a compartment rear of the driver's cab."

"Good work, Bob, get the team together – we'll move on Turner tomorrow."

"Whoa! There's more, Matt!" Dixon's voice was serious. "Forensics found traces of explosives in the floor dust."

Loader, suddenly alert, shrugged off the problems pressing in on him.

"Oh my God! Change of plan! Hold everything! Forget chasing Turner. We need more intel before we stir up a hornet's nest. We need to get advice on this, Bob, for God's sake keep a lid on it until I get clearance."

"Will do – it's still in the container! I'll kill the reports and we'll release the van, accept the driver's explanation and send him on his way."

Loader closed the call then immediately called Nigel Phillips, Head of Covert Operations, MI5.

Together, they decided that both the home secretary and the secretary for defence must be brought into the loop. Nigel said he would call an urgent meeting.

"Matt, you've got a hell of a lot on your plate right now with the SETI implications – shall I get Dixon to take the lead on this?"

Loader realised he was under pressure and working all hours but felt, somehow, the two stories were intertwined.

"I'll stay in situ on this, Nigel. Anyway, Bob Dixon is doing the grunt work, but I want to keep tabs on the whole picture. Please set up the meeting; I'll front it."

An hour later, Loader received a return call from Nigel.

"Right, Matt, I've spoken with both home and defence secretaries. This is being added to the COBRA agenda next Wednesday. You'll have to be there and take the MI5 lead."

CHAPTER 20

The fourth COBRA meeting to be held in as many months was chaired by the prime minister, Grace Armstrong.

"This is unprecedented, I know," she said, "but we are entering unprecedented times. I need all departments to be on high alert with immediate effect. There are two items on the agenda. They may or may not be linked. MI5 have uncovered serious information that you all need to be aware of. We'll take the first item.

"Next week, the UK Government is going to release information that will shake the world. It is not just any story, or even a global story, but one which is of cosmic importance. We must release the story of the UK astronomer Mr Newby's discoveries to the public, as signed protocols require us to do. But the Brown Bear files remain under our Official Secrets Act and will not be linked, or leaked, to any source.

"It is not difficult to imagine the potential surge of public reaction. Will there be mass hysteria? Will there be mass demonstrations? Does the news represent a threat to our country? As you know, we are already receiving a growing encirclement of Russian assets around our shores – will they take advantage of the furore to mount an even more aggressive incursion? Colleagues, we must be alert to every imaginable scenario and be prepared for it. There is already a growing public anxiety about alien sightings. Other governments, too, are taking the matter seriously."

She paused, nodding to the defence secretary, Malcolm Bishop. He took the lead. "In light of our advance info to them, the US Government is preparing to relaunch a team of UFO hunters. Our own MoD-dedicated UFO desk was disbanded in 2009, since when no agency has been responsible for monitoring the skies over Britain for unidentified flying objects.

"However, depending on the findings of a Pentagon UFO report, which have been renamed Unidentified Aerial Phenomena, UAP, there is every possibility that the department could be revived. The constantly evolving nature of emerging science and technology can suddenly open up whole new universes, and this is exactly what may be happening now, and it is important to ensure the UK does not lose sight of the need to identify and track objects in space and our airspace.

"Currently, RAF Fylingdales tracks objects in space and is our current means to work with the US and others. We do not have any other role in the US task force, and although we are aware of the planned report, we have not contributed to it. This is something that will change. If there's something unexplained in our airspace, we want to know what it is, particularly when it's been seen from time to time by our own pilots and tracked on civil and military radar. So, let us prepare for next week."

Grace Armstrong surveyed the room of cabinet ministers and security agents, who were sensing dramatic times ahead.

She went on. "The second concern is closer to home, and it's probably not connected to the first item at all, but the two seemed to have become interrelated. Mr Loader."

Loader took the cue. "Thank you, Prime Minister. As you are all aware, there's been a covert Russian group in the UK for a number of years. It seemed to have been disbanded soon after the Salisbury incident, but a few months ago, a signal was intercepted by GCHQ, reactivating it. The cell is known as Brown Bear. Only two operatives were thought to have remained in the UK – we have tracked them down and now believe the cell to still be operating."

Loader went on to describe the events leading to the Turners Express Couriers and the discovery of explosives residue. He paused, as if debating what to say next.

"Prime Minister, ladies and gentlemen, I have been in this business for a long time. What we are uncovering may be some minor terrorist threat, but my gut is telling me something else. We all watch the news; I am concerned that there is a much bigger threat on the agenda, that the ground may be being prepared for a major assault on our country."

A loud muttering of voices broke out.

"Be more precise. What are you getting at?"

"OK. It is only conjecture at this time," Loader responded. "We have all attended COBRA meetings and learned of the ever-increasing belligerence of rogue states, and I include Russia! We've learned of Russian incursions towards sovereign territories, not just our own! They are hell bent on expansion, control of the Arctic, aggressive moves towards Baltic States, the invasion of Ukraine, the threat and movement of nuclear assets..."

Grace Armstrong, watching Loader with calculating eyes, broke in. "I understand what you are saying, Mr Loader. What we must do is to focus on the here and now. There are two active situations which could have global implications, and we are caught up in both. I want to see the formation of small, dedicated task groups and agendas to keep a close grip on these events. I want this government to be fully spatially aware of any fallout from these topics.

"I suggest that the home secretary and the defence secretary, together with the security services, are best placed to lead the task groups. Given your involvement, Mr Loader, I believe that you should be the focal point for both groups."

It was not a request. Her look circled the room.

"I'll take questions."

CHAPTER 21

Loader was basing himself with Susan at the farmhouse, preparing her for the media turmoil that was sure to erupt following the publication of the 'Newby Discoveries'.

Somehow, there was already a tense expectancy within the media, although no one quite knew what.

The global syndicated copy would be released on Monday at 6am for publication on Tuesday. First issues of the *Telegraph* would be out before midnight on Monday.

At the moment, secrecy was being held together tenuously by a combination of D-notices and the Official Secrets Act. This latter applying specifically to the Brown Bear project.

The D-notice, more accurately known as a DSMA-Notice (Defence and Security Media Advisory Notice), is issued by an independent (of government) body housed within the MoD. These were advisory notices which the media in general adhered to. Media organisations did not want to run the risk of being blacklisted on new stories emerging.

Only two days to go, by Monday night, the world would awaken to a new story in the history of the universe and of mankind.

Susan viewed the preparations with alarm.

"It will only be for a couple of weeks," Loader explained. "Once every other scientific establishment have the facts and their own facilities in place, the interest in this location will ease, but meanwhile, we need to keep this place safe from chaos."

"So many people here."

"Well, yes, I'm afraid so." Loader was beginning to feel the stress mount.

Newby's work had been corroborated by the RAS, but Loader knew that his career was still on the line. The idea of aliens in space communicating with the earth was the stuff of science fiction. Suddenly, fears of a major hoax were real again. What if this was a gigantic scam at the expense of the UK Government? Thankfully, Grace Armstrong had steered the media release to be that of Newby's discovery, no more – it was left to the public and institutions to make of it what they will.

But Loader was taking no chances. He set up a three-shift security team to control the entrance to the property and patrol the boundary of the farmhouse and field. He brought in a partner, John, for Claire, to provide close protection to Susan at all times.

He added another housekeeper and cook to the staff tally.

Jenny agreed to provide RAS technical support for the observatory, now the office and control centre.

Loader showed the additional security team around the property, so they had intimate knowledge of what they were protecting. By the end of the day, everything was in place. He took a walk round the farmhouse and into the field where three mobile accommodation containers had been parked. He went back to the house and joined Susan in the living room.

"I think we're all set now," he said, adding with light humour, "the sun is over the yardarm; can I get you a drink?"

"Please." She managed a smile. "I've been talking to Claire about the working arrangements for the new staff. It all seems so strange! Only a month or so ago, there was just me and George rattling around here. Now it's full of people. The annex has been taken up and the fifth bedroom."

"It's difficult, I know, but in a couple of weeks, I hope everything will return to normal."

"You seem so sure of everything, Matt; I don't know how on earth George would have coped if he hadn't met you."

"Right place, right time, I suppose. He could have simply just announced his findings and sat back. But this way, he is controlling the story and making a fortune in the process."

His mobile phone buzzed.

"Loader," he said, then listened intently. "Thank God! Is he up to visitors? What? OK. We'll be there in the morning."

Susan looked at Loader, a mixture of query and hope in her eyes.

Loader took a deep breath. "George is conscious!" he said, a grin of relief spreading over his face.

Susan clasped a hand to her mouth.

"Oh! Matt!" she cried and burst into tears.

Loader went to her and hugged her close. Eventually, her sobs died away; she disengaged herself and dried her eyes.

"Did you say we can go and see George tomorrow?"

"The consultant said not before lunch, so we will get there about two ish."

He called Claire in. "Great news, Claire. George is conscious. Would you please take Susan to the hospital tomorrow morning. I'll follow on later in the day. Fix up some local overnight accommodation for yourselves."

After supper, Susan went to bed early, tiredness etched on her face.

Loader went into the observatory; he stared at the monitors which, at this time of night, were in receiving mode. He was beginning to feel at home here, looking with familiarity at the signals dancing on the screens. He got to thinking about the story to be released onto the unsuspecting world. He wandered out to the antenna room and stood on the plinth steps looking into the cloudless night sky. Night-time was still cold at this time of year; he stared into the astonishing Milky Way, billions of stars stretching in an exuberant arc across the sky as far as the eye could see. Each little dot of light coming from a star system billions of miles away. He felt he could see forever.

He mounted the plinth steps and put his eye to the sighting 'scope. There was a profusion of dots around the periphery of the lens, but the focal centre stared out into an abyss. Was there really an intelligent life force out there looking back along the sight line, thinking, living, sending signals to earth? His mind turned to Susan's concept of intelligent life. He saw that for twenty years, while George was single-minded, working on his electronics and optical systems, Susan had been left alone to ponder on the meaning of life. Theirs had been a strange marriage, one of convenience. He saw the loneliness in Susan's eyes and his heart ached for her.

Just Sunday to go! Then she and George would be thrust into the limelight and a media-driven frenzy. He was sure of that. He went back inside to the observatory; somehow, the ethereal static from the room filled with electronics receiving and processing energy from distant space, seemed to calm him.

Too late now anyway. The die was cast.

CHAPTER 22

It was almost mid afternoon on Monday before Loader was able to get to Basingstoke hospital. He hurried along the corridors to Newby's room, stopping only to speak briefly to the guard outside the door. He stepped quietly into the room.

Newby was propped up in bed, his eyes closed, plasma drips and oxygen assist masks attached; he looked aged and frail. Susan was sitting at the bedside, head drooped, asleep.

Loader stood for some moments gazing at them both, then he spoke quietly.

"Susan." Then a little louder. "Susan!"

She woke with a slight start, her face lighting up with relief at seeing Loader.

"Matt!" She half stood; Loader quickly crossed to her side and held her close.

"How is George?"

She sat back into the chair. "Well, he's sort of conscious. He opened his eyes and I'm sure he recognised me. I hold his hand and there is a slight response. I don't know, it is all so horrible. The consultant comes in every hour."

"What does he say?"

"Just that we need time."

Loader looked at Susan's drawn face.

"You must be at your wit's end," he said. "Today is the day, Susan. George's life's work will be global news tonight. There is a lot of anticipation, and tension in diplomatic circles. I'm so sorry that I have to come and go, but I'm going to stay with you here until we see how everything evolves and unfolds this evening.

"Look, how about a stroll and some lunch. Then we'll come back and see how George is. I have arranged a large TV screen to be brought in, then if George is able, he can watch the breaking news himself. It may stimulate him."

They left George sleeping and went to find the on-site restaurant.

"Matt, this is all so much to take in; I don't know how I would have coped without you."

"You don't have to cope without me." Loader tried to lighten the tone. "I've a lot to gain too. The articles I've written are quite lucrative."

"It's more than that; there's more to what you are doing. You seem to be involved in so much more."

"I admit there will be a lot going on over the next weeks and months, and you will be part of it, Susan. You must take credit for your long dedication to the project. And while George is unwell, you will be the focus of the story."

"I didn't ask for this, Matt."

"I know, but it is recognition, and you will be in demand."

"It's George's project; I'm not sure I can stand in for him."

"You will manage, Susan. You've been part of all that George has done, and I'll support you all the way."

"I know," she said simply.

They finished their lunch and took a walk outside to get some fresh air, then headed back to see George.

He was awake, a nurse checking his monitors. As Susan appeared in his line of sight, George's eyes registered her presence, following her movements.

A large screen TV was set up at the foot of the bed, ready to show the evening's news.

Below them, on the ground floor, a meeting room had been commandeered as a temporary operations and communication centre; some twenty TV monitors were set up, tuned to all the major international broadcasters.

Loader and Susan chatted quietly, sometimes including George, but he remained very sleepy.

It was coming up to 5pm; Loader took a call on his mobile, his face impassive while he listened. After a few minutes, he acknowledged the caller and terminated the call.

"There's a change of plan," he told Susan quietly. "That was my boss. The Cabinet believe that we are unable to keep the lid on things much longer; there's already some speculation leaking into the mainstream media. In this day and age of twenty-four-hour online news reporting, it's almost impossible to maintain rigid news discipline. The PM is to make an announcement and a press release at six o'clock."

They instinctively looked at the wall clock – it was 5.10pm.

Loader switched the TV on to BBC News. There was a documentary about national gardens, no hint of the breaking news to come.

Downstairs in the communications room, TV monitors were tuned into all the global news stations, infeed from satellite-enabled equipment in vehicles parked outside.

At 5.30pm, the BBC announcer broke into the programme.

"We're interrupting this programme to inform viewers that there is a major breaking news item to be broadcast at six o'clock. The prime minister will address the nation." The TV gardening programme resumed, to be interrupted every five minutes until it was abruptly terminated at 5.55pm. The TV switched to the Downing Street briefing room. A senior BBC presenter filled in time trying to speculate what the newsflash was about.

Promptly at 6pm, the prime minister of the United Kingdom, Grace Armstrong, came into the briefing room and stood at the lectern. Two Union flags were draped on the wall behind her.

Grace Armstrong, poised and calm, did not appear to have any notes. She looked directly into the cameras and addressed the nation without preamble. "This evening there will be an unprecedented press release of global and historic importance. I want you all to be aware of its background. What you will learn is that a British astronomer, Mr George Newby, has detected astonishing radio signals of extraterrestrial origin. The received energy detected by Mr Newby contains codes which are indisputably created by an alien intelligence source." She paused, allowing the significance of what she had said to sink in.

"As you will imagine, when this was first reported, it was greeted with incredibility and cries of 'hoax'. The signals must have somehow been generated on earth and beamed onto the astronomy radio telescope. With these thoughts in mind, Mr Newby's findings were given rigorous testing over a period of three months by expert witnesses in the astronomy field and finally corroborated by the British Royal Astronomical Society.

"It is the view of all who have examined the data that the signals *are* extra-terrestrial and further, that they contain evidence of intelligence. With the press release this evening, the British Government passes all findings into the public domain for further examination and comment. If proven correct, the news may have severe implications for us on earth, good or bad.

"I leave it for international scrutiny to determine authenticity and possible outcomes. Meanwhile, I can inform you that the UK Government has called for a meeting of the United Nations to discuss the protocols and actions to be taken, if any.

"Finally, I pay tribute to the British astronomer George Newby and his wife Susan, who have dedicated years of their life to reveal this remarkable phenomenon. Please be assured that all future developments will be fully reported to the public and the media."

Grace Armstrong smiled at the camera and, with a slight nod, turned and left the room. The camera turned to the presenter who sat silent for some seconds before rallying himself to close the session.

Immediately following the prime ministerial announcement, all national news TV channels cleared their schedules for the next twenty-four hours. Senior presenters were called in to catch the earliest press releases. Meanwhile,

TV programme producers were frantically trying to gather appropriate interviewees to take up the story.

The presenters struggled gamely to fill the gap, with speculation and postulation.

At last, at 8pm, the *Daily Telegraph* newspaper finally received security clearance to release the news. Instantly, the copy was flashed around the globe to over fifty syndicated news channels, the *Telegraph* itself posting a digital version on its website.

The first print editions were beginning to roll off the press in an atmosphere of feverish excitement. The international news networks headlined their reading of the syndicated story even before they had prepared the scripts:

'Email from an alien world!'
'You are not alone'
'Radio signals from a billion years ago'
'Intelligent life contacts the earth!'

And so they went on, playing for time, scrambling to get a script put together before the headlines to come.

The *Telegraph*, as the information source, had the full story instantly available on its website; soon after 10pm, the first print editions were available on the newsstands.

A small group had gathered in George's room: his nurse, who was asked to stay, Loader, Susan and both Claire and John. They gathered either side of the bed, careful not to crowd it, watching the unfolded breaking news. Susan sat holding George's hand and communicating to him in soft tones and hand squeezes. George himself seemed to become aware that something was going on, his eyes on the TV screen, occasionally a slow look around, then his eyes closed for a short time.

The BBC News presenter cut away from a side dialogue and looked into the camera.

"Well, here it is! We have now received the full news release of this extraordinary story set out in the first editions of the *Daily Telegraph*."

The TV cut to a full view of the *Daily Telegraph* front page. Beneath the banner was a colour picture of the night sky, the blackness lightened by the bright dots of a billion stars and the fuzzy smudge of distant galaxies. The Milky Way arced over all in a glorious sweep across the sky.

Just the bottom quarter of the page was devoted to the opening texts.

Loader noticed that George had opened his eyes, staring at the screen. The presenter showed the spread of the second and third pages. Top left hand was a small head-and-shoulders photo of Loader, his name below and the caption '*DAILY TELEGRAPH* SECURITY AND DEFENCE CORRESPONDENT'. There was no other mention of him throughout the length of the twelve-page article.

What did take up most of the spread were photos of British astrophysicist George Newby MA. PhD and Susan Newby MA. PhD, together with a view of their home and of the radio antenna, shown stark against a darkening sky.

As the presenter took the viewers through the evolving story, George's eyes followed every move, the corner of his mouth taking on an imperceptible smile; he sighed gently.

As midnight approached, George had fallen asleep; the nurse took over and the visitors quietly left.

"George knew what was going on," Susan said when she and Loader were alone.

"Yes, I noticed that too. It is good that his life's work has been acknowledged and that he knows it."

"What do we do now, Matt?"

"Well, here? Just a watching brief. At the farmhouse, the TV companies are moving their trailers to the orchard and setting up there for a while. I would like to be at the farmhouse too until some assessment of the world's reaction is made and we can see the next moves."

"Perhaps everything will just die away, and people will get on with their lives."

"Maybe. I suggest you stay here for a day or two with John and Claire and we'll see how George gets on. Dixon is reorganising security at the farmhouse and I need to get to London for breakfast. There's a lot of follow-on work to be done for the articles."

"You will come back to the farmhouse though?" Susan's voice sounded anxious.

"Yes of course. I'll keep in touch every step of the way. Now, don't forget you'll be in huge demand for a few days; Claire will keep everyone at bay until you feel up to giving interviews."

"OK," she said.

CHAPTER 23

There was breaking news as Loader got to the *Telegraph*'s offices.

Moscow's defence ministry said that it had fired warning shots at a UK warship and that SU-24M warplane had dropped bombs close to the vessel. The UK defence secretary insisted that the warship had been aware of Russian training exercises in her wider vicinity ahead of conducting a routine transit through the Black Sea.

Russia considered the route to be part of its territorial waters, although Britain does not recognise the claim, rejecting Moscow's illegal annexation of Crimea in 2014. A BBC journalist embedded on the warship describes the ship as being harassed by the Russian military. He said that twenty Russian aircraft and two coast guard vessels were shadowing the warship as it sailed close to the south-west coast of Crimea.

Reports described hostile warnings coming in via radio and the warship crew manning action stations preparing for a potential confrontation. Two Russian patrol ships tried to force it to alter course; at one stage one of the Russian vessels closed in to within about one hundred metres.

Loader read all the available reports and the background to the published 'international rules for the traffic separation scheme (TSS)'.

This sort of cat-and-mouse game was a common occurrence, but the opportunity for a misjudgement was huge.

In response to a request, Loader was able to speak to a MoD source.

"Is it correct that the destroyer had been called to action stations?"

"Well, yes. That is a standard response in any drill," the spokesman said.

"But this wasn't a drill, and I understand munitions were actually fired."

"We took it as a drill and reacted accordingly."

"Did the destroyer actually target the Russian planes?"

"The captain would follow protocols, and at some stage, it may include having the opposite number in the ship's sights."

"But," insisted Loader, "had the destroyer received any damage, would it have fired at the Russian plane?"

"As I said, there are protocols; some would require release from the Government."

"That's a 'no' then?"

CHAPTER 24

Late that evening, Loader returned to his apartment intending to drive to Norfolk the next morning.

At the hospital, Claire and Susan had left George sleeping and retired for the night. The TV was turned off; the security guard sat in the hall reading.

It was at 2am when the bedside alarms went off. The guard dropped his book and raced into George's room; he stared at the flashing alarms, unsure of what to do. Within seconds the staff nurse came running along the corridor and into the room, straight for the monitor screens. She turned off the sound and pulled back the covers to attend to George. Two more nurses arrived.

"Cardiac arrest!" the staff nurse called in a clear, calm manner. "Prepare defib!"

She fussed at George's bedside, clearing his oxygen mask and bearing his chest. A few more checks, then, "Ready defib."

The guard stood back, helpless, as the duty consultant also arrived.

The sound of the defibrillator smacked into the room, followed by resuscitating compressions and checks.

"Again!" the nurse ordered, the process repeating. After three attempts, the consultant took over. Examining vital signs, he stood back. "He's gone," he said simply.

Loader took the call from Claire at 5am.

"Matt, I'm so sorry," she said.

Loader immediately knew.

"How is Susan?" he asked.

"Tearful but very calm. John and I will sort things out this end and get Susan to the farmhouse later today."

"OK, Claire, thank you so much for your care to Susan."

"Of course," she said. "You think a lot of Susan, don't you, Matt?"

He didn't reply.

"She's a lucky lady to have you watching her back. See you later then."

"Thank you, Claire." Loader rang off. Too late to go back to bed. He made tea and sat mulling over the ramifications of the news.

He was at the Norfolk farmhouse by midday and set about checking the organisation of the enlarged staffing, updating everyone regarding George Newby.

"Mrs Newby will be returning here tonight," he informed them. Turning to the housekeeper and the cook, "Please help ensure a calm welcome for her."

He went into the observatory to check on the preparations being made by the RAS staff assigned to assist. The president of the society, Jenny, was herself there.

"We've received numerous requests for visits and for presentations," she said.

"I'm not surprised," Loader replied. "I'm happy that you set up a schedule of future visits, but please delay until after Mrs Newby's affairs are sorted out."

Early evening, Claire called. "Ten minutes away," she informed Loader.

He paced around the living room, suddenly uncertain of how to react to Susan. He went to the front door and waited for her car to arrive.

Claire was first out of the car, offering a hand to Susan. Seeing her, Loader was consumed by competing emotions. Emerging from the car, she looked momentarily at the house and Loader in the doorway.

Her face was impassive, pale, but seemingly composed. She was wearing a blue dress, under a light jacket, a picture of elegance. Clearly, she had similar uncertainties as Loader; their embrace was restrained and slightly awkward.

Loaded covered his uncertainty with trivial questions. "Welcome home, Susan. Journey straight forward?"

"Thank you, Matt." Her voice was neutral. "Everything is in order, but I admit I'm quite tired."

They went together into the living room.

"Coffee or wine?" Loader asked.

"Thank you, a glass of wine would be fine."

"I fixed some supper for eight o'clock tonight if that's OK?" he said.

An hour later, after a second glass of wine and mundane chat, the awkwardness lessened, and they were able to talk about the situation.

Susan fiddled with the stem of her wine glass.

"I'm sure George knew what was going on and was

pleased that his story was at last told. Once he saw the news on TV, he seemed to relax," she said.

"You're right, Susan. George's lifetime's work has been recognised; he knew it. What we must do now is to build on it and carry it forward."

"We?"

Loader paused in confusion. "I'm sorry, Susan. I didn't mean to presume. It's down to you, of course. But there has always been a security issue mixed up here, and I need to tie things up officially, before bowing out."

"*No*, Matt! I'm very happy with 'we'. I want you to stay on and for us to work together. I just wanted to know if you meant it."

"I very much meant it," Loader said, anxious to return the conversation to safer topics. "But you have got to plan for the future. There are loads of people clamouring to meet you. Earlier today, Jenny took a call from the director of the Carl Sagan Center, SETI Institute, in California. She wants to send a small team over to meet you and look at the observatory."

"This whole thing is getting overwhelming. George and I were so excited when we realised that we had contact with an alien source, we didn't realise the media and political storm it would create."

"You must have guessed," said Loader gently. "It's the biggest event in the history of this planet."

"Yes, but it's George's work. I know a lot about what he was doing, but I don't have the technical knowledge to discuss the details."

"I know. Jenny has brought in an electronic expert to study George's diagrams and to understand the digital processing." Loader paused. "Look, let's sleep on it and get together with Jenny in the morning to sort out a schedule."

Susan sighed. "OK, and tomorrow Claire is going to help me to sort out funeral arrangements; I'm thinking it will be early next week." She stopped, staring into the distance.

The next day they spent in the observatory. Two more desks and some chairs had been added into the cavernous barn.

Jenny and the electronic engineer used one; Claire and John sat at the other.

Susan and Loader worked from the large central table.

Loader had spoken with Claire. The security issue had subsided, and she and John would not be needed any longer in that role, but would they consider joining the staff in a management role? They both accepted and took over the logistic planning for visiting groups.

Jenny continued to field the flood of queries from organisations wanting to know more about the radio telescope.

Jenny got on well with Susan, who was content to let her organise the technical aspects of George's work and even proposed that the whole subject be known as the 'SETI UK project'.

Later, back in the private office in the house, Susan and Loader were sifting through the pile of post which seemed to arrive by the sackful.

"Here are two more royalty bank transfers," Loader said. "You have become a very wealthy lady these last few weeks."

"Mmm."

"Do you have any idea what you want to do?" he asked.

"Not really. I shall have to give up this place, perhaps gift it to the Astronomical Institute."

"The George Newby Observatory?"

"Yes, that sounds good."

"What then?"

"I don't know, Matt, I shall concentrate on what I've always been interested in, basically neuroscience. Astrobiology is very interesting too, but I've always been fascinated by the mind/brain function."

"I'm a bit lost here, Susan, what are the differences?"

"I guess the astrobiology route is sexier; I could get work easily in that field. Also, I've got a PhD in psychology and so have a bit of a head start. But what I really want to do is to find out what we are. Have you never thought about it? Our brain is an organ, and there are many studies into how it works, but it is not who we are any more than your lungs are what you are. It's the mind that fascinates me, not the ailments and fixes for mental aberration but how it works. What are we, Matt? What is the unique 'you' which controls everything? For example, what is it that makes you choose to do something or go somewhere, without any specific external trigger?"

Loader exhaled loudly. "I suppose you could study both?"

"Well, yes, and I've already had some experience, such as doing research in a lab and lecturing at a university."

She paused, then added mischievously, "I could do the same as you, work in a press office informing the media on the latest happenings, or as a science journalist writing about the latest discoveries in websites, magazines, newspapers or books."

Loader grinned. He looked across the table at Susan. Talking about her own passion had returned some colour to her cheeks and even a sparkle in her eyes.

"We could be a team," he said. "Loader and Newby, investigative journalists."

"Or Newby and Loader."

"'L' comes before 'N'," he parried, still grinning.

Susan looked at him, pouting. At that moment, she looked absolutely adorable. He felt a surge of emotion and, to cover his confusion, raised his hands up, palms out.

"OK, I give in."

"You didn't fight very hard," she observed, getting up from her chair. "Must be time for a cuppa?"

The two representatives from SETI arrived, Dr Stella Watson and Professor John Deacon. Both serious and quietly spoken.

Loader had arranged for them to be brought to Norfolk from Heathrow by helicopter. He was in the field to greet them. Ducking away from the rotors, their baggage unloaded, they waited until the helicopter had departed and the noise level returned to normal.

It was a short walk through the rows of portacabin offices and accommodation that had sprung up.

"We've put you in the house," Loader said, after introductions.

Susan was at the front door.

"Ha! Susan Newby," Stella Watson said, with outstretched hand. "I recognise you from your photos, which seem to be in every magazine in the world at the moment."

"Hello, welcome to the farmhouse," Susan responded, with a light smile.

"John Deacon," said professor Deacon, taking Susan's hand. "Thank you so much for allowing us to visit so soon.

Our condolences too; it must be very hard for you."

"Thank you," Susan said quietly. "Please come on in. Leave your bags in the hall; I'll get them taken up to your rooms." They all moved through the hall into the main living room, grouping in front of the large French windows looking out into the orchard.

"Now, what would you like to drink?" There was a side table with coffee, crockery and hot water set out.

Formalities over, everyone relaxed, discussing the journey and the differences between Norfolk's weather and California's.

Claire entered the room; Susan ushered her forward.

"This is Claire, part of our team. She will show you to your rooms to freshen up, then we'll have a light lunch before we get down to details."

Following lunch, the party went through the hall to the observatory. Entering the large barn, both Stella and John Deacon stopped abruptly in amazement.

"Well!" said Stella. "I didn't know what to expect. I was thinking the whole thing was going to look like a homespun project, but this! Well, it's surprising."

She and Deacon paused, taking in the huge room with four sides of the walls taken up with racks of electronics, floor to ceiling.

They stared at the huge monitors mounted on the back wall, alive with recorded waveforms. Loader ushered them gently across the room, still gazing around, to the door into the antenna room.

Out in the roofless room stood the three-metre dish on a scaffolding mount, angled to the sky. Several equipment housings took up floor space, drive motors, head amplifiers and transmitter installation.

"I'll be darned!" John Deacon exclaimed. "I never thought I'd see anything like this."

"Over twenty years of dedicated radio engineering," said Loader. "I, too, was overwhelmed, but then I knew nothing about radio astronomy; I didn't know what to expect anyway."

"Well, this is unique," Stella said, walking to the base of the antenna mount, looking up at the sighting 'scope. She then wandered to the far wall and the missing windows, taking in the view of the field and the Portakabins below. Susan joined her. "The field is where George built his first Yagi array but soon dropped it and concentrated on microwave horn feeders into the dish."

"I'll be darned!" said Deacon again.

They returned to the observatory. Loader had asked the representatives from RAS to join them. After introductions, they sat around the large table. Susan took the lead. "This is where George spent most of his life and where SETI Man was first discovered some ten years ago."

"SETI Man?"

Susan smiled at Stella. "Well, yes. When we first received the signals, we didn't know what to make of them. I mean, how long had these signals been beamed to earth? What did they mean? At first, we jokingly referred to them as our 'little green men'. But then, after the latest experience, and Matt's involvement with your organisation SETI, we started to refer to the signals as SETI Man."

Deacon gave a wry smile. "OK. SETI Man it is. I would be interested to go through the signal processing circuits with your expert here, but first, can we look at the actual received signals?"

Susan nodded. "We'll come back here after dinner, about ten o'clock, when the telescope is aligned with SETI Man. What I can show you now is the recorded waveforms from last night."

She indicated the monitors on the wall. "This waveform is the raw signal received through the antenna."

They all looked at the screen. Looking up, they saw an oscilloscope waveform of what looked like noise dancing across the screen.

"Yes, it looks like a typical cosmic noise pattern," said Susan. "But after signal processing, the waveform can be analysed for properties such as amplitude, frequency, rise time, interval, distortion, et cetera. George discovered the intelligence when he was trying to explain sudden shifts of phase. Which brings us onto the next image."

She switched the monitor picture.

"Now you see the same waveform but expanded to capture a shorter timescale. This is where George discovered the phase shifts. He put a marker each time the phase shifted and found the repeating sequence. One phase shift, gap. Two phase shifts, gap. Three phase shifts, gap. Four phase shifts, long gap, then repeat. This was the eureka moment in George's life. That was ten years ago." She stopped abruptly, her eyes welling up.

Loader quickly diverted attention. "At that time, George had no idea how long those signals had been arriving. Months? Years? Also, he had no idea where they came from. But he then spent a year developing the transmitter. It was eight years after he started to send his response, which mimicked the original, except with the progression two, four, six, eight. He deduced that the source was four light years away. Very close by astronomical standards."

"Indeed," Deacon commented.

Stella asked gently, "When George discovered this ten years ago, why did he not make it public then?"

Susan had regained her composure.

"At first, he was afraid of ridicule, that it was some form of hoax. He wanted to be absolutely sure before he announced it to the world. He was also, by nature, a loner and was trying to establish a contact before he went public. When he did get a response six months ago, he was ecstatic, but we had run out of money and were in a lot of debt. That's when he finally decided to go public and approach Matt and the *Daily Telegraph*."

"Take us through the response of a few months ago," suggested Deacon.

"Well, that was the craziest day of our life. George just couldn't believe it, and even then, he had an undercurrent of fear that it was hoax."

Susan put the latest response on the monitor. The red markers showed verticals in groups of two, four, thirty, eight, sixteen.

"It took a few seconds to sink in," said Susan, but I quickly saw that the thirty was the sum of the progression.

"It's odd that the thirty appears in the middle of the sequence. It would seem obvious to put it at the end, a sum," Stella commented.

"I believe it contains two messages. The first is telling us that they have picked up our transmission and understood it. Secondly, and it's my own interpretation, by placing it in the centre of the sequence, it's a message that SETI Man is on his way here."

Susan lifted her chin as she spoke, as if daring anyone to argue.

Stella looked thoughtful. "That needs thinking about. It seems a big stretch to make that interpretation. Let's talk more when we look at the actual telescope viewing tonight."

After dinner, they all met in the observatory: two SETI representatives, two RAS members, Loader and Susan.

They started by examining the antenna positioning, then into the observatory. Susan faced the group, her back to the large screen.

"What you see here are the actual microwave signals picked up from the antenna, mixed to an intermediate frequency, then processed through pulse length and occurrence discriminators and, finally, frequency and phase demodulators."

Everyone gazed at the vibrant waveform dancing across the screen. Around the walls, the equipment panels showed a variety of green and red indicator lights; a faint but distinct hum and static seemed to fill the room.

Loader still didn't understand the technical jargon that Susan used, but it clearly resonated with the SETI group. Susan went on.

"The radio telescope alternates for fifteen minutes between receiving and transmitting modes." She paused as the visitors began to ask questions.

It was past midnight before the visitors proposed to retire.

"We'd like to stay on tomorrow if that's OK," Deacon said, as they cleared their files.

"Of course," Susan agreed. "Let's go into the kitchen for a nightcap before you retire."

"I'll stay on for a while and check everything is secure," Loader said.

The group left, still chattering about the significance of the cosmic signals. Loader went into the outer antenna barn. It was a perfect night for stargazing: dark, chilly and a clear sky. He strolled to the far side and stared up into the night sky. His mind drifted as he stared upwards. The night sky had become very familiar to him following his association with George and Susan. He searched out well-known stars and constellations, but always his eyes were drawn into the depths beyond the cloudy haze of the Milky Way. He tried to see the Andromeda Galaxy, the nearest major galaxy outside the Milky Way, comprising of over one hundred million stars. He imagined he could make out its distant smudgy glow with his naked eye. What was really out there? He envisioned other worlds, maybe primaeval, and now maybe even with intelligent life. His mind pondered an intelligence unencumbered within a physical body. Lost in reverie, he jumped at the voice beside him.

"Matt, what are you doing over here?" It was Susan seeking him out. She stood close by his side and saw that she had startled him.

"I was, well, I was just looking at the stars."

"What were you thinking, Matt?" she said softly.

Her closeness, casual clothes, perfume, hair tied back in a girlish bunch unsettled him; he felt excited. He made an effort to remain objective.

"I was thinking about the wonder of it all, the spiritual

power at work. I just feel there is something more out there than we'll ever know," he said lamely.

"Maybe we're going to find out," Susan said, seeking his hand. "Come on, Matt, it's chilly out here, and I've got fresh coffee in the kitchen."

CHAPTER 25

Susan wanted George's funeral to be a family affair, but it was not to be. His name was now known to almost every living person in the world.

Family amounted to less than five relatives on George's side and three on Susan's side. They all expressed a desire to attend his funeral which was planned to be a low-key committal at the local crematorium. There was no cortège planned. Susan was taken aback by the demands of the world's press to attend the committal service and from ex-colleagues from George's academic days. Even from names not familiar to Susan, who wanted to pretend in some cases, thought Loader, to be part of the fame that now attributed to George. The astroscientist who discovered life in the voids of space.

The crematorium chapel was full and overflowing with press contingents in every part of the crematoria and grounds.

At 9am sharp, George's coffin was wheeled respectfully into the chapel, where committal proceedings were followed by eulogies from George's relatives and from a student-days colleague who told the world about George's belief in extraterrestrial intelligence and his single-minded quest to discover it.

Later, at the wake – held in a marquee in the field of the farmhouse – so many people wanted time with Susan. Loader's heart went out to her, besieged by people she hardly knew. She remained calm, elegant in a midnight-blue dress, hair tied back, a lightly veiled fascinator hat.

Loader stood in the background, scanning the throng of mourners and press.

His eyes suddenly alighted on a woman standing in the background, quietly watching the proceedings. Liz! The home secretary. He weaved his way through the throng.

"Home Secretary!" He smiled. "It's good of you to come; I had no idea!"

Liz seemed pleased to see a face she recognised.

"Ha. Matt. Liz, please! I felt someone should be here to represent the Government."

"Come over and say hello to Susan; she'll appreciate it." They made their way to where Susan, beginning to look a bit hunted, was still besieged. Loader broke into the group around her.

"Susan, you remember Liz?"

Susan smiled in relief to see them. Liz inserted herself effortlessly into Susan's orbit. Loader watched the tension ease from Susan's face.

Catching Liz's eye, he mouthed 'thank you' and moved on.

The following day, every newspaper headlined the funeral of George Newby, the British astronomer. There were column inches of his days as a lecturer in astroscience, then self-imposed dedication to searching for extraterrestrial intelligence.

The press had also picked up on George's abduction and apparent poisoning, linking to the ongoing court case of the two Russian spies accused of his attack.

A picture of Susan featured prominently, summarising her own academic achievements and role in supporting George's work.

One headline blazoned: 'SUSAN NEWBY PREDICTS THAT ALIENS ARE ON WAY HERE'.

CHAPTER 26

Loader returned from London. Claire greeted him at the front door of the farmhouse.

"Susan's in the observatory," she said. Loader thanked her and, dropping his bag in the hall, went through to the barn.

Susan was on her own, engrossed in her laptop. The monitors were active, showing the processed signals; as usual, an air of static filled the room.

She jumped up from her chair as Loader entered.

"Matt!" she said. "I wasn't expecting you until later." She came forward for a hug.

He grinned mysteriously. "Well, now, I've got some news! How are you? I see no one is here today."

"Nope. Things have quietened down a lot this week; I've been able to have the place to myself for the last couple of days."

"I'm not surprised. It's a month today since we broke the news, and the media have been full of SETI Man for weeks, but I think people are beginning to have had enough; other things crowd in. Anyway, to celebrate one month, I'm going to take you to dinner tonight at the best restaurant in Norfolk."

"Matt, wouldn't you rather stay in? You've just driven up from London; you must be tired."

"No. I've planned it, made the reservation already."

Susan's eyes shone with pleasure.

"I've not been out for… well, since… I can't remember." Her face fell.

"What's up?" he asked anxiously. "You'd rather stay in?"

"Well, no it's just that…"

"*Wait*! Say nothing," he commanded, reaching in his pocket, fishing out a small piece of paper and handing it to Susan. On it was written: 'I've got nothing to wear!'.

"That's what you were going to say." He laughed. She joined in.

"You are horrible, Matt."

"Not at all. It's a standard saying all girls make before going out."

"How do you know?" she asked severely.

"I read it," he replied. "Anyway, this might help." He handed her a package which he brought in with him.

Susan opened the bag, taking out an elegant dress.

"Matt! It's lovely," she exclaimed. "How do you know it'll fit me?"

"I own up! I got Claire to get it for me yesterday."

"It's really beautiful." She held it up against herself. Loader watched her posing, smoothing the fabric down against her hips.

"This is lovely news," she said.

"No. That's not the news, Susan, something better."

"Tell me then, Matt, don't keep me in suspense."

"Right, well, I received a call from Liverpool Twickenham Studios. They want you to sign a film rights deal."

Susan was dubious. "I don't think I could face telling the world about my life."

"You won't have to; your story is already well known, and you would be played by a proper actress!"

"Matt!"

The next morning, Loader travelled to London. He would be there for most of the week.

The first meeting was with the CSA and Dixon.

The following day he spent with the defence and security agency preparing a brief on SETI Man for the United Nations subcommittee prior to airing at the General Assembly which was now an agenda item for the September meeting.

The remainder of the week was taken up with press briefings and releases regarding defence and security issues. He spent some time in discussion with the editors of the *Telegraph*.

He received a call from Deacon, the SETI director.

"Hello, Matt. I thought you might appreciate a heads-up on a press release due out tomorrow. How are things going at the farmhouse?"

"Hi, John, good to hear from you. Things are settling down a bit now. Public attention seems to have been diverted to climate change issues. Although we still get regular reports of sightings of UFOs!"

Deacon chuckled. "Ah, yes. We do too! Look, Matt, one of our CARMA millimetre wave observatories in California has been retooled and has reported picking up the SETI

Man signals." Loader could picture Deacon smiling as he used the term.

"That's fantastic," he said. "That means we will get an official endorsement of Newby's work."

"Well not yet, we are still building the signal processing circuits. It'll be a week or so yet, but at least they've identified the signal. There are still problems in agreeing on the source; I mean, there's no obvious formation that could produce this at the distance we calculate."

"Four light years?"

"Yes. It's too close! Anyway, there will be an advance notice released tomorrow. You'll get a copy directly from us."

"That's great, John, appreciate it. I'll bid for column space as soon as I get the copy. Look forward to seeing you over here again before long."

"Me too." Deacon rang off.

Loader immediately called Susan to give her the news.

"I'll be home tomorrow," he concluded, pausing awkwardly, suddenly realising that he had referred to the farmhouse as 'home'.

Susan picked up on it too. "It'll be good to have you home, Matt," she said.

Loader wanted to say more. Instead, he merely said, "See you tomorrow then."

Susan was not at home when Loader arrived at the farmhouse.

"Susan has made quite a lot of changes while you've been away," said Claire as they took coffee in the kitchen.

"Oh? I'm pleased that Susan is finding her feet, so to speak. So, what has changed?"

"Well, the police were here on Monday. They feel that it would be appropriate to remove the police presence here. They said there is no longer an overt risk. Susan agreed. On the police recommendation, she called in G4S who have upgraded the alarm system over the whole site. We now have just one security man here on a three-shift basis."

"OK. That makes sense."

"Susan has also offered Alec, the electronics guru, a full-time role to maintain the equipment. We are getting requests for visits from all sorts of people and institutions. Several local astronomers have agreed terms to act as demonstrators. It's been hectic, Matt, but everything seems to have settled down quite well."

Loader nodded. "Excellent, and we are lucky to have you and John to manage the project. Susan could not do this alone – the whole thing would just fold."

Claire looked at Loader. "She's got you, Matt. She thinks a lot of you. Anyway, John and I have accepted permanent roles to run the farmhouse as an educational project. Susan's got some ideas she wants to explore. The housekeeper and chef are staying on too, so everything seems good."

Loader agreed, then went off to the observatory to chat with John. A group of visitors were expected that evening.

John explained that the group were staying at the local hotel and would be on site after dinner, 9.30pm until past midnight. He added that he had an arrangement with the hotel and that all visits were arranged on packaged commercial terms.

Loader wandered back to the living room, gazing out at the fields beyond.

The intercom announced the arrival of Susan at the main gate. He was out at the front door to greet her. Emily and Tracey were with her.

Susan came to him for a greetings hug.

"I'm sorry I was out, Matt, I've invited Tracey and Emily over for the night, is that OK?" she asked anxiously.

Loader held her close for a second, absorbing her fragrance, softness.

"Of course, Susan. It's your house! Good to see Emily and Tracey again."

She relaxed. "And I've got some news, later"

He turned to Tracey and held her hand.

"Lovely to see you again, Tracey, we'll have a good chat later. I expect Emily wants to have a look at the stars!"

Tracey, anxious at first, warmed to Loader's smile.

She wore a simple blue dress over her slight frame, with white ankle socks and blue trainers. Shoulder-length hair fell straight, framing an attractive, oval face, permanently wary.

Emily stood back, oblivious of the introductions going on around her.

"Hello, Emily," ventured Loader. "Remember me? I'm Matt, Susan's friend." Emily looked at her mum, then at Loader; he detected a glimmer of recognition but didn't pursue it. He followed the ladies into the house.

Afternoon tea with cake was served in the living room.

"News?" said Loader in mock interrogation.

"Ohh, yes! Matt, a group of scientists have invited me to join them and lead a research project at the Norwich Research Park."

"Wow, Susan. That's amazing. What's the project?"

"It's a neuroscience project. There has been an informal grouping for some time, but SETI Man has accelerated their decision to formalise a project – I'm really excited."

"I'm so happy for you, Susan." They chatted on.

Tracey asked permission to take Emily into the kitchen and beg some cake material from the housekeeper for Emily to mix at the kitchen island.

On their own, Loader and Susan sat in companionable small talk.

Later, after supper, Susan took Emily through to the sighting telescope. It was still a bit too light, but just dusk enough for Emily to be satisfied.

Loader sat with Tracey in the living room. She sat on the edge of the seat, obviously unaccustomed to making small talk.

Loader gently coaxed information from her. She was twenty-nine with no formal education and little prospects for a job.

"Emily takes all my time," she said defensively. "Even at twelve she can't be left alone for long, so I'm a sort of full-time carer." The defeated look returned. Loader could understand the despair of having nothing, and no prospects of change, in addition to the physical exhaustion of looking after Emily.

"Do you get any time to yourself?" he asked gently.

"Well, yes – Emily goes to the hospice several days a week."

"So at least you get some rest." It was a clumsy statement which he quickly regretted.

"Rest! No, I have to get part-time jobs to help the benefits."

"So, no time to yourself at all?" He tried to sound sympathetic, non-condescending.

"Well, sometimes Emily takes a turn and just flakes out."

"What can you do when Emily is 'flaked out'?"

"Write."

Loader lifted his head in surprise.

"Write?"

"Yes." Tracey backed off in embarrassment. Loader quickly got her back onside. "That's what I do, Tracey. Did Susan tell you?"

"No, I didn't know."

"What sort of things do you write about?"

Tracey said nothing for a few moments.

"Things around me," she said deprecatingly.

"That's great. I write about things too but mainly foreign stuff. What is it that interests you most?"

Loader's tone was engaging, Tracey saw no threats of ridicule.

"Well, things going on, nature, weather and the dangers around us."

"Dangers, Tracey?"

"I think things are going wrong."

"That is ever so interesting. Do you show it to anyone?"

"Oh, no I couldn't!"

"Why not, Tracey?"

"Well, I, I don't count."

Loader felt a surge of emotion for the young girl, a soul trapped in the web of circumstance.

"Of course you count, Tracey. Believe me, you count very much. Come on, let's go and see what Susan and Emily are up to."

They stood up to leave the room; as they went through the doorway together, it seemed natural that Loader took Tracey's hand.

The evening class of amateur astronomers had assembled around the large table in the observatory. Loader spent a few minutes chatting to them.

He saw from the corner of his eye that Tracey was sitting with Alec who had draped an arm across her shoulder.

Loader went into the antenna room; Susan and Emily were sitting on bistro chairs on the far side of the roofless barn, both reclining and staring into the now dark sky.

There was no artificial light anywhere, the whole panorama of the heavens suspended in the glory of a billion dots of light scattered in profusion from one horizon to the other. The diaphanous swathe of the Milky Way stretched in an exuberant arc across the sky.

Susan turned to Loader and Emily.

"Every time I look into the heavens, I see more and more," she said.

Emily had not moved, transfixed, her hands cupping her face.

Loader pulled up another chair, joining in the stargazing.

Staring into the sky at night was mesmerising. As Loader strove to see further and further, his body felt irresistibly drawn towards the void, infinite, timeless.

They sat quietly for some time, absorbing the grandeur, the immensity.

Loader murmured quietly, "It's astonishing to know that out there, so far away, is an alien intelligence that has contacted us. I wonder what they look like?"

No one ventured a reply.

Eventually, the spell was broken by the astronomy class spilling out into the antenna room to look at the radio dish and to look through the sighting 'scope.

It was a lovely evening. All too soon, it was time to think about bed.

The following day, Susan took Tracey and Emily back to their hostel. Loader spent time on zoom meetings with the team preparing the file for the UN meeting.

He received a call from Deacon.

"We've got the modulated signals," he announced. "Identical to the patterns we recorded at the farmhouse. We're discussing a project to transmit back to the source."

"Has anyone thought about Susan's interpretation of the signal pattern?" asked Loader.

"Oh, yes of course. Just about every institution in the States is looking at it. There is some support, but in the main it's discounted."

"Really? I back Susan on this one!"

"Of course you do, Matt," Deacon said drily. "Oh! NASA has also entered the field. They' re directing a sizable part of their deep space effort into this search."

They rang off, promising to keep in touch.

It was now late August. Loader was due back to Norfolk by the evening. Briefs had finally been completed for the United Kingdom representative to the UN Assembly in New York.

Tracey and Emily were staying over.

Susan was in the final stages of preparing opening positions for her new project due to start in four weeks' time.

She worked at the large table in the observatory, looking up from her papers as Emily appeared in the doorway, carrying her astronomy book.

"Hello, dear. Do you want to sit outside?" Susan said, referring to the antenna room.

Emily held her book in one hand, her elbow and wrist held at a strange angle.

She said nothing, her other arm fully outstretched and pointing to the antenna room door.

"OK then, come along." Susan got up and guided Emily to the chair near the optical telescope.

Emily sat, ignoring her book, just gazing ahead.

Susan paused, looking at the child with a heavy heart. She could see that Emily was struggling with a headache. Her faced was pinched, eyes narrowed.

She wanted to gather her in her arms and comfort her, to assuage the pain, but she knew it would be rebuffed and could bring on a tantrum.

Alec joined them. He made a pretence of adjusting the sighting 'scope, then looked into the eyepiece. Emily watched him warily. Alec then indicated that she could take a look. There was little response but, with a smile and outstretched hand, Alec finally got Emily to the sight, and she peered into the night sky.

After a moment, she turned to Alec with a huge grin. "Stars," she said.

Alec laid his hand gently on her shoulder. "Yes, stars," he murmured to her.

It was four days before Loader could revisit.

He made good time and arrived at the farmhouse before

lunch. In the kitchen, Claire made him a coffee; he took his briefcase and the coffee through to the living room. Tracey was sitting on the patio outside, reading a local magazine, something she could not afford at home.

She looked up as Loader appeared, a fleeting glance of apprehension before guarded relaxation.

"Susan said we could stay for the day," she said defensively.

Loader smiled, joining her on the patio.

"Hi, Tracey. Can I get you a coffee?"

There was a moment's confusion on her face, as she grappled again with a response to kindness.

He went off to the kitchen and asked Claire if she could rustle up another coffee for Tracey. Back on the patio, he asked how Emily was.

"She's in the telescope room," Tracey replied. "She's got a headache this morning. I'm hoping it will go away before I have to medicate her."

"And you? How are you?"

She shrugged. "Quite good, thank you."

"Oh! I bought you a little pressie in London yesterday." Loader pulled a zip file case from his briefcase. "I thought you might like this." He offered the gift to Tracey. She stared incredulously at the file case, her eyes filling. She took it almost gingerly as if it would vanish in her hands. Unzipping the top, she took out a loose-leaf A4 book, the cover pronouncing 'Artists and Writers Notebook'.

She gazed at it, riffled through the pages. Such a simple gift, but it overwhelmed her; her eyes welled, a tear escaping down her cheek. Loader reached for her and held her close.

"Just for you to practise your writing," he said gently, trying to lighten the moment. She saw something else in the folder and took out a pouch filled with pencils and felt-tip pens.

"Thank you so much, Matt." She sniffed, drying her eyes with the back of her hand.

Loader steered the conversation to generalities. They discussed holidays, which she'd never had but had always dreamed of visiting the coast and just taking in the scenery.

They were interrupted by a crash and muffled cry coming from the observatory.

Loader leapt to his feet as Susan burst into the room.

"They're here, Matt! They're here!" She rushed towards him, in a state of near panic.

"Whoa. Calm down, Susan! Who's here?"

"SETI Man, Matt. SETI Man! They're here now!"

Loader felt a steel band tighten around his chest. Her eyes were fixed on him, her face excited, frightened, eyes wild and sparkling with an iridescent light.

Reaching her, she caught his arm, "SETI Man's here!" she cried again then, eyes rolling up, she fainted to the floor.

"Oh my God. Susan! Susan!" Loader panicked as he knelt beside her, holding her head off the floor.

"Susan, are you OK? Look at me," he commanded, smoothing her cheeks, entreating her to respond.

He grabbed a cushion off a chair and placed it under her head. He felt her neck for a pulse.

"Tracey! Go and get Claire. Quickly!" he shouted.

She was crying, looking frightened, but rushed off to the kitchen.

Claire arrived. Her training as a CPO included managing medical emergencies.

"Let me see!" she commanded, easing Loader to one side and kneeling beside Susan.

"She has a good pulse; breathing is heavy and a bit jerky."

Loader was agitated. "I'll call for an ambulance."

"Just wait a moment. Let's get her onto the settee and make her comfortable." Tracey stood in the doorway, transfixed.

Claire gesticulated to her. "Go and find John, *now*!"

Tracey turned and ran off.

They made Susan comfortable on the settee; Claire checked that the neck of her blouse was not restricting her breathing.

"She's out cold but seems to be OK," she assured Loader. "Vital signs OK and I notice rapid movement of her eyes. I think she's just fainted. I'll go and get some water and a flannel."

Loader knelt on the floor beside Susan, holding her hand, his voice anxious.

"Susan, please wake up. Can you hear me?"

He caressed her hand, the steady rise and fall of her breast indicating steady breathing. He looked at her face in repose, longing for the life and smile to return.

"Susan," he said again. "Come on! Please wake up." Then, overcome with fear and emotion, he whispered, "Susan, I love you. Please wake up."

Suddenly, it was in the open, even if she was unable to respond. He loved Susan!

Claire returned with a bowl of water and flannels, taking Loader's position beside Susan.

He paced around the room in agitation. "We've got to get the medics."

"Just wait a short while, Matt, before you jump the gun. People faint for all sorts of reasons. Susan is warm and comfortable and breathing steadily; her heartbeat is strong; let's just wait a bit."

Loader continued pacing.

"OK. You stay with Susan. I'm going to find out where Tracey has got to."

He hurried through the hall into the observatory, stopping short in the doorway. John was at the big table, slumped forward. In the corner of the room, at the monitor desk, Alec, the electronics engineer, was lolling backwards in his chair, arms dangling to the floor, as if he'd been trying to get up before collapsing.

There were sounds of wailing coming from the antenna room. Loader dashed across the observatory.

Tracey was kneeling at a chair near the optical telescope clasping the lifeless form of Emily, weeping uncontrollably.

"No!" she sobbed. "My Emily! Please no."

Loader rushed forward to help. Tracey fought him off. "No! It's my Emily," she cried.

"Yes, of course, Tracey. Let's just get her somewhere more comfortable." He gathered Emily's slight form into his arms and, with Tracey still attempting to fend him off, carried her through the observatory into the living room, Tracey clutching at both of them.

Claire leapt to her feet as he entered.

"Emily is out too and John and Alec!" Loader spoke urgently, as he gently laid Emily in an armchair. Claire quickly checked Emily for heartbeat and breathing.

"Same as Susan," she said. Tracey continued to cry over Emily's still form.

Loader paced the floor. "What the hell happened in there? Something spooked all of them. I can't move them into here; we need help!"

Claire hurried into the observatory room to examine John and Alec.

Loader called the emergency services.

Within the hour, three ambulances arrived at the farmhouse, 'blue and twos' dying as they pulled up. Six paramedics met Loader at the front door, rucksacks in hand.

"The casualties are in the living room," Loader stated as he led the way.

"*Four* casualties?" the lead medic queried.

The medics quickly and calmly examined the four patients, then confirmed Claire's earlier diagnosis.

"They didn't pass out in here. So, what happened?" asked the lead medic.

"No, they were working in our observatory and suddenly just passed out."

"All four?"

"Yes."

"Odd. Let me look at the scene of the – er – accident."

Loader led the way into the observatory. The medic looked around the room in uncomprehending amazement.

"And they were just sitting at this table?"

"Yes, working on some papers. The little girl, Emily, was in the antenna room next door."

"Hmm! Seems odd to me, all four collapsing at the same time, no obvious reason."

Loader didn't go into the SETI Man aspect.

"I'll have to call it in," the medic said.

The patients were stretchered into the ambulances and driven off at a more leisurely pace to the county hospital.

Their departure left a sudden anticlimactic feeling, an emptiness. Loader and Claire sat in the kitchen working out what they needed to do next.

"What happened in there?" he asked yet again.

Claire looked nonplussed; the corner of her mouth turned down.

"God knows. We ought to shut the telescope off, until we know what happened."

"No! Claire. If indeed there is any link between what happened and the so-called SETI Man, is it safe to break the link until we know the patients are safe?"

She looked alarmed. "So, is there an alien influence at loose in the observatory? Is it confined to the room, or…?"

"I don't know, Claire, but breaking the transmissions could be fatal to the patients; we must see how they are and what they can tell us when they come round."

"If they come round," Claire said, forebodingly, her imagination running riot.

Their deliberations were interrupted by the G4S security duty guard announcing the arrival of a senior police officer.

The newcomer was accompanied by a uniformed police officer.

"Mr Loader? I'm DCI Fletcher, Norfolk Constabulary. We've been called in by National Health England to investigate the circumstances of four people struck down at this location. I have a team on their way here now. I trust we can rely on your cooperation." It was a statement not a question.

Loader nodded. "Of course. Come in and tell me what you need."

"Thank you." The DCI followed Loader into the living room; Claire was there – Loader introduced her.

"Right. Thank you, the team will be here shortly. Meanwhile, I'd like to take a look at the site of the, er, accidents." The DCI paused. "You are *the* Mr Loader, the newspaper reporter who seems to be at the centre of all the events regarding the alien story?"

Loader glanced at Claire. "It gets complicated," he said. "Let's just get you started on your investigation."

It was less than eight hours since Susan and the others passed out at the farmhouse.

Emily and the two men were placed in adjacent wards. Tracey sat glued to Emily's side.

Now, Loader stood at Susan's bedside in the hospital, explaining the events to the attending consultant.

"Well, I know of the Newby Observatory, of course, and the story of SETI Man, it's the talk of the country. As far as the patients are concerned, I can find no explanation for this. There is no trauma; all the vital signs are about normal, although the heart rate and breathing are slightly up, temperature too, very slightly. We're taking blood samples and making further tests. It is possible they have passed out due to a shock of witnessing something, but that would be very unusual."

Loader thanked the consultant for his attention.

"Can you please ensure that no drugs of any sort are administered in an effort to bring them to consciousness until we know much more about their condition."

The consultant nodded. "Of course, there's no need for that anyway at this stage, but if they are out for long, we'll have to consider IV infusion and catheter."

He briefed the attending nurses before leaving.

The ward fell silent; Loader could just hear Susan's steady breathing and was reassured. He spent the rest of the day by her side, taking short breaks to check on the other patients.

Tracey remained by Emily's side. She herself had sunk into a lethargic state of despair. Even absorbed by his own fears, Loader sensed the despair that, after years of selfless devotion to her ill daughter, and despite being alone and penniless, the young mother's anguish at the thought that she might lose the one precious thing in her life.

He returned to Susan's ward and sat again at her side. The night wore on. There was no change in her condition.

The morning routine began. Loader needed to go to the farmhouse to shower and change clothes. There was also some 'office' work to attend to.

He held Susan's hand again before leaving, telling her where he was going and promising to be back later that evening.

Susan continued to lie motionless; her only sign of life was her chest rising and falling gently.

He left his contact details with the attending nurses with strict instructions to alert him should there be any change to Susan's condition. He checked with Tracey. She did not want to leave.

Loader drove to the farmhouse. Security was back on the main gate. The housekeeper was in the kitchen with Claire, who had also driven back from the Norfolk and Norwich Hospital.

Loader went straight to his room to shower and change. Refreshed, he picked up a coffee from the kitchen and, after chatting to the housekeeper for a short time, asked Claire to join him in the observatory.

The first thing he did was to call Deacon, in California.

"Do you know what God damn time it is?" a sleepy voice muttered.

"Sorry, John. This is urgent. Matt here, by the way. We've got a situation here. Yesterday, Susan and three others in the observatory fell into a coma."

The voice in California suddenly became alert.

"What do you mean exactly?"

"Just that! Susan was working the in the observatory and came running into the living room, shouting, 'They're here, the SETI Men!' Then she just passed out. She's in the county hospital now, with the others."

"Who?"

"John and Alec and a little girl, Emily, that Susan has befriended. She was in the antenna room near the sighting 'scope."

"What's happening to them?"

"That's what's odd. They seem OK. Vital signs OK, just in a coma, unresponsive."

"Are you thinking it is anything to do with the radio 'scope?"

"What else can it be? Anyway, it is galvanising the authorities here to investigate. We've got a meeting here on Thursday. With the medical and security reps. I wondered if you'd like to join by Zoom?"

"Yes, I can't make it in person, but Zoom is good. Send me joining instructions."

They rang off.

The electronics were all on in the observatory, as they had been, twenty-four seven, for years. Panel lamps gleamed. The large monitor screens displaying cosmic noise received through the radio telescope. Loader remembered when George had shown him the audio output, and they had listened for a short time to the eerie sizzling sound, like a frying sound, Newby had said.

Loader and Claire sat at the large table.

"You OK?" Loader asked.

She nodded, sipping her coffee. She had coped well to the events of the past twenty-four hours but looked tired.

"Thank you for all you've done, Claire, and for handling things so well. Now, we've got to find out what the devil happened here. I've not got a clue."

Claire nodded. "It's got to be something to do with all this." She looked around, indicating the banks of electronics with her arms.

"You're right, and this is what concerns me. Did something shock them somehow? What struck them down? Anyway, I'm bringing the security back up to scratch tomorrow to watch the site. Also, I've got Dixon to send you a partner, Mike, until John's back up and running. So perhaps you would both attend the meeting on Thursday."

Loader made more calls. Both the home office and the RAS would send someone to the meeting.

CHAPTER 27

It was ten days since Susan's admission. Loader was back in the hospital. She, and the other patients, remained unconscious. He entered the ward quietly, going to Susan's side to hold her hand for a while. She remained motionless on her back, eyes closed, breathing steadily.

"There is little we can do," the consultant had said. "While all vital signs are positive, we can only wait. We have tested every parameter, including a brain scan, everything is correct. There is quite a bit of brain activity. As I've said, we can only wait. Absolutely the best help is your presence here. Touch her; speak to her. It can only help to bring her back."

"Susan, I'm here," Loader pleaded, caressing her hand gently. "Everything will be OK."

He continued chatting to her, quietly updating her on everyday trivia, steering clear of the growing hysteria about SETI Man in the media.

Susan was connected to yet more monitors and aids. On day two, she had started intravenous feeding and a catheter was connected. Through it all, she lay unresponsive.

Loader sighed deeply, gently releasing her hand. He moved to a corner table and chair that had been arranged. Opening his laptop, he scanned the article he had mapped out the day before, following a brief given by the chief of staff.

He read it again.

Continued testing of Russian underwater nuclear drone, Poseidon, *threatens stability of the Arctic*

The Poseidon, *a Russian nuclear-powered, nuclear-tipped, underwater mega-drone, is undergoing testing and development in northern Russia, in areas of the Barents Sea, White Sea, Kola Peninsula and Novaya Zemlya.*

Nuclear submarines like the Belgorod *and the* Khabarovsk, *designed to carry* Poseidon, *are currently under testing and construction at the yards in Severodvinsk.*

Nuclear activities in Norwegian neighbouring areas constitute a significant risk, Norwegian intelligence reports.

In response, Russia claims NATO has changed patterns from normal patrols and intelligence gatherings in the areas, to simulated attacks on Russian targets, including with strategic bombers. Part of the Russian narrative is that introducing new areas of warfare, like the use of digital operations and militarisation of the space, is potentially being used to attack Russian ballistic missiles before launch. Thirdly, Russia blames the United States for undermining the global security balance and arms control treaties, and thereby pushing the world towards a new nuclear arms race.

It was also hinted that should Russia face the prospect of being defeated in a conflict with NATO, the use of tactical nuclear weapons could be an option.

The Norwegian Intelligence Service rejects the above listed misguided narrative that NATO is causing insecurity.

In its annual intelligence report spelling out the shift in policy, it said: 'Russia has no self-imposed restriction on non-first use of nuclear weapons'.

Moscow, however, considers an undermining of the strategic balance as an 'existential threat' that could justify the use of nuclear weapons.

Nuclear warheads are stored at a large national-level facility on the Kola Peninsula and at several smaller base-level facilities.

These storages hold many nuclear warheads, both non-strategic and strategic nuclear weapons, according to a Norwegian intelligence report.

Transport of nuclear warheads by train and on road pose a risk of incidents that could cause releases of radioactivity.

Loader addressed the email to Jan, *Daily Telegraph*, and pressed 'send'. It would appear in the paper tomorrow.

The silence went on. A nurse came and went, briefly breaking the monotony. Loader returned to the bedside, gently lifting Susan's hands into his own.

"I'm still here," he said softly. "We'll be OK, just come back to me, Susan – please!"

He went on, talking in generalities, the anxious best wishes from her new research team; the project was due to launch in two weeks' time.

He had got a gardener in to tidy up the flower beds around the farmhouse.

Tracey was looking after Emily, spending all her time at the hospital.

Loader had agreed that, when this was over, they should both stay at the farmhouse indefinitely.

The UN General Assembly was due to meet in New York in three weeks' time.

Loader continued to talk to Susan. "You never did take a holiday, Susan. That's what you need, a holiday. I'll come with you, and we'll lounge somewhere in the sun and just relax with no agenda. How about Cyprus? I've been there. You would love it."

There was no response; Susan lay motionless, only her regular breathing showing signs of life.

Over the days, she had grown pale and had lost weight.

Dejected, he returned to his desk, listlessly looking through incoming emails. He was very tired; he closed his eyes for a moment, the silence wrapping around him. He imagined he heard a quiet voice from the bed.

"Matt?"

He sprang to his feet – it was real! Susan had turned her head towards him. Her eyes were open, gazing at him steadily.

"Matt," she repeated softly.

It was the most euphoric moment that Loader believed his name would ever evoke.

He moved quickly across the room, then slowed before

reaching the bedside; he approached her gently. There were tears in his eyes.

"Susan, my Susan," he whispered, placing his hand on hers. "You're back. I've been so frightened, wondering what had happened to you."

Susan moved her head slightly, eyeing the oxygen supply, the drip, the heart rate monitor, the catheter; she said nothing, returning her gaze to him, her face in repose but her eyes studying his face.

"I'm going to call for help, to make sure you're OK and comfortable," he said and, reaching up to the console, pressed the panic button.

Two nurses came into the room, fast!

Loader motioned with both hands, palms down, slowing them abruptly.

"Susan's with us," he said simply.

The nurses approached Susan smiling and, with gentle voices, began to assess her status. Some minutes later, the resident consultant arrived. "The others are conscious too," he announced, then introduced himself to Susan before looking through the notes completed by the nurses.

"I can find no adverse signs. I want her to remain here for some time yet. Meanwhile, we shall start to remove some of this plumbing," he said, indicating the support systems with a wave of his arm.

Loader left the nurses to do their work and went to the restaurant for a coffee.

The first person he saw there was Tracey. She came forward, throwing herself into his arms.

"They said Emily is going to be OK," she sobbed. "Oh! Matt, it was horrible."

Loader consoled her. He was again moved by the young girl's desperate concern for her daughter, even knowing the child's prognosis.

Entering the restaurant, Claire caught sight of them and joined in the relief and tears of joy.

"John and Alec are awake," she said. "I can go back in an hour when they've given them some tests and a wash-up."

"Right. Let's sit down, I'll, get some coffees; something to eat would be good too." Loader took orders and went to the counter.

Later, Loader returned to the ward. Susan was alone; the wires and tubes had been removed; her eyes were closed but opened as he entered.

"Susan!" he said gently, approaching her side. "Are you feeling better now?"

She said nothing, her eyes following him. He sat beside her, hand on hers.

"I've been so worried about you," he said.

There was silence for a minute.

"I know." Her voice was soft, steady.

"Susan, I didn't know what to do!"

"Mmm."

"Susan, I love you."

"I know."

"I've always loved you."

"I know."

They sat in comfortable silence for some time. Susan closed her eyes. Now she opened them.

"I had a dream," she said softly. Loader waited a beat.

"Do you want to tell?" he asked.

"It was like lying face down in a warm swimming pool, my legs and arms outstretched, except it wasn't water. I was naked and sort of floating in space. It was space, Matt, but I was not cold and I could breathe. I was comfortable. Everything felt warm, happy. My eyes were open; I was staring into the heavens below me, Matt, I could see the stars, the galaxies, and I felt the eternity of space between them, but I couldn't recognise the constellations.

"One of the heavenly bodies drifted towards me, or I moved towards it, I don't know, but as it drew closer, I saw it was a world. And as I came closer to its surface, I realised it was our planet earth; I remember little of it except a feeling of peace and happiness."

She paused. Loader wanted to ask questions, but he kept silent. After long moments, Susan continued. "I couldn't make out what was on the surface, but it seemed very ordered and sunny. Things were going on in my head, a sort of tinnitus, I just felt that I had no control; I was a witness, no more. Then the view below began to change; I began to get impressions of the surface. I saw, in the distance, huge fires burning. Then the surface moved below me, or I travelled across it, I don't know. Images came to me from the surface. I saw men fighting, whole towns in flames and destruction. As I moved across the surface below me, I caught glimpses of flooding. Large areas devastated, cars piled on top of one another, houses destroyed. I could see many areas of the globe, and further scenes of war; there seemed to be scenes of conflict everywhere, gangs, murder and fighting.

"It was horrible, Matt! I wanted to get away, but I couldn't, I seemed to be travelling over the surface of the globe, transfixed, seeing outbreaks of horror everywhere. I saw…" Susan drifted into silence. Loader waited.

Eventually, Susan's voice continued softly, "Then the globe sort of drifted away into the darkness, leaving me staring again into the vault of heaven, billions of stars spread out before me in profusion and splendorous wonder. I felt peace again, a warmth and comfort; I can't remember any more."

Susan stopped talking.

Loader tried to assimilate the scenes conjured up in his mind. He could visualise them in the context of press reports, many by his own paper, the *Daily Telegraph*.

Put together, the scenes pictured a world heading towards Armageddon, conflicts and climate disasters that were likely to destroy the world.

"That's weird, Susan," he said. "I wonder what triggered a nightmare like that? And knocked you out too."

Susan said nothing.

"By the way, just before you passed out, you shouted that SETI Man was here. What did you mean by that? We found nothing in the observatory."

Susan turned her full gaze to Loader.

"SETI Man is here, now!" Her voice was a soft whisper. "The incomprehensible 'signal' from the radio telescope is the fundamental energy source carrying SETI Man."

Loader was sceptical. "We didn't see anything."

"No, you wouldn't. Matt, I believe that SETI Man inducted itself into my brain and into the others who fainted too."

Loader sat in stunned silence, then said gently, "No way, Susan. This is the stuff of science fiction. Probably, the warmth and static in the observatory got to you, and the others who were there too, and you just fainted."

"Yes, I know. But ten days in a coma! How do you explain that?"

Her voice tailed off, tired. Her eyes closed.

He squeezed her hand gently. "Well, it's over now; the nightmare is gone and you're here with me. Get more rest; I'm just here."

They spent the rest of the day together; Susan slept most of the time. Now and again, she surfaced; Loader was aware of her eyes staring at him, inscrutable. In the afternoon, the consultant returned, accompanied by nurses. Loader left them to go through their monitoring regime, waiting outside.

It was nearly an hour later that the consultant emerged. Loader stood up expectantly.

"All the signs are good," The consultant announced. "However, I want to keep Susan under observation for another day, but tomorrow she can get out into a wheelchair and be taken for some fresh air. Then the day after, we shall need to begin extensive tests. We need a first-hand account of their experiences, which we'll do on Thursday. They may remember more if we arrange a group get-together."

Loader grinned with relief, returning to Susan's side.

CHAPTER 28

Sixteen people gathered in a hospital conference room of the Norwich Research Park, which had been commandeered by Loader. The meeting was due to commence at 10am.

He had arrived there an hour before, ensuring that the Zoom facility was up and running. The chairperson of the Royal Astronomical Society was present. As was the home secretary. Deacon would join at 10am by Zoom. Claire, Tracey and Dixon were present. Six senior consultants were also in attendance.

With fifteen minutes to spare, the three patients, Susan, John and Alec, arrived in wheelchairs. Coffees and biscuits were provided, and non-essential staff quietly withdrew.

At 10.05am, the attending consultant entered the room, his face serious. "Ladies and gentlemen, there is an issue with Emily; she will be delayed. The meeting will reconvene at 11am."

Tracey leapt from her seat with a moan of anguish and rushed towards the door. The consultant caught her arm gently and escorted her from the room.

Loader cut through the babble of voices that followed the announcement.

"Right!" he said loudly. "While we are waiting, let's go through the proposed agenda, and I remind you that the purpose of this meeting is to collect and collate the individual experiences of our patients here." He nodded towards the three wheelchaired patients. "We shall be recording your personal stories and hope that by recounting these as a group, it may tease out forgotten detail. We need to find out what happened and why. Perhaps this session will help the experts here." He looked towards the consultants.

There were some questions as the room filled with general chatter.

11am. The door opened; all eyes turned. The consultant stood inside the doorway, his face shocked.

"Ladies and gentlemen, I apologise for the delay. I don't know what to say to you all! I cannot understand what has happened. Following initial preparation for this meeting, Emily exhibited signs that were abnormal to her. There was an emergency call-out, culminating in a trip to the MRI scanner. Colleagues, I just don't know what to say! The MRI scan was double-checked. Emily's tumour is not in remission! *It's gone!*"

There was a loud gasp from the assembly; everyone talked at once, and as the consultant stood aside, Emily entered the room in her wheelchair, pushed by a radiant Tracey.

Emily was a different child. No longer awkward and slack-faced. She looked at the assembly with alert eyes and a slightly self-conscious childish grin. Everyone started laughing in joy and clapping. Tracey went to Alec;

reaching his side, she hugged him as he reached up from his wheelchair and wrapped his arms around her waist.

Loader looked on, his heart going out to her. At last, it seemed that her life held a future.

It was some time before order was restored. Claire gathered Emily to her, both laughing and crying at the same time. The consultants gathered around the attending consultant as he gave an account of the tests made on Emily and of his total bafflement. Eventually, the buzz subsided, and Loader was able to take the chair.

"Thank you all! This is all astonishing and not comprehendible! We are so relieved to have our patients back with us again, and Emily's recovery is miraculous. Now we need to find out what happened in the observatory that evening. What caused our patients to pass out, and what did they experience? So, I would like to ask each patient to recount everything they can remember about what they were doing at the time. Did they see anything? Feel anything?

"John, you were in the observatory at the controller. Would you start us off? Where were the others? And please tell us what you think happened."

John nodded.

"So, well, I was looking at the latest recording of the evening's signals. Just looking for any aberration, I guess. Alex was across the room at the processing console. Emily was in the antenna room, as always, just gazing through the sighting 'scope. Susan was opposite me, working on some thesis she was preparing. The room was, as usual, quite warm. With the light from the three active screens creating a sort of stroboscopic effect. I recollect that the background noise was on.

"I definitely felt a presence. It came suddenly; I saw that Susan and Alec felt it too, because they both looked up with startled faces. It wasn't scary or anything like that, but it was eerie. I felt excited. Then I had a drowsy feeling, feeling strangely comforted, and then somehow, I was leaving the room, not walking, but I just seemed to visualise moving away. Then I remember losing all thought of the observatory and instead was in a city; I don't know which. Then I was in several scenes: cities, villages, meetings. Scenes which were in a blur really, a kaleidoscope of colours and sounds. The next thing I remember is waking up in hospital."

One of the consultants asked, "Did you have any sense of feeling? Pain, say, or touch."

John grimaced, trying to think back. "No, nothing specific. I did feel a sort of caressing, as if warm air was blowing gently over me."

Another consultant asked, "Was there any speech or voices?"

"No, there were no voices, but I did feel as if someone was with me. I could sense a sort of gentle murmur, comforting hum really. I remember that the murmur grew more stressed as I saw bad scenes."

Loader asked, "Bad scenes?"

"Well, yes. Some city images were often scenes of bombed-out apartment blocks, piles of burned-out vehicles, rubbish strewn everywhere."

"Do you know where you were?"

"No, but they looked like the places I've seen on TV, Ukraine and that."

There was a silence as the meeting tried to visualise John's experience.

Loader said, "OK, John, thanks for that. We'll probably come back with more questions later."

He turned to Alec. "Your turn, Alec. What do you remember?"

"Much the same as John, I think. Although I seem to remember more about scenes of rubbish. There seemed to be an indescribable amount of dereliction and rubbish strewn everywhere. Often there were groups of people sitting around, homeless like. I got a sense of deprivation."

"Do you know where you were?" asked a consultant.

"No, not any specific place, but as the images came and went, I could see it must have been worldwide. I do remember feeling depressed; I seemed to have feelings I didn't recognise, as if I was in a seance."

"What sort of feelings?"

"I felt sad, looking at the scenes of destruction, of rubbish everywhere, of men carrying weapons... I don't know, I just felt so frustrated of man's capability to trash his environment and destroy his fellow men."

There were a few more questions about Alec's experience.

Susan told the audience of her similar experiences. Although having seen similar scenes, her overriding sense was one of a love and compassion that seemed to envelop her.

Then all eyes turned to Emily. Facing the room full of people, Emily's newfound confidence was wavering.

Loader stepped in, smiling. He brought her attention to himself. "How are you getting on with your book on astronomy?" he asked gently.

Emily's focus was brought back to something in her comfort zone.

"It's great," she said. "I've looked through it loads of times."

"And you like looking at the stars through the telescope?"

"Oh yes! I can see everything; it's beautiful."

"You were looking through the 'scope when you fell asleep, weren't you? Do you remember anything special?"

Emily's brow knitted. "I remember I was trying to see Saturn and its rings."

"What happened?"

"I suddenly felt someone behind me and then cuddling me."

"Weren't you surprised?"

"No, I don't think so. It was warm and gentle; I thought it was Mum."

"How sure are you it was Mum?"

Emily hesitated; it seemed an odd question to her. "Well, she sort of cooed and whispered in my ear; it felt like Mum."

"OK, Em – that's great, thank you. What happened then?"

"I don't know. Mum seemed to worry about something and cuddle me some more, and I fell asleep."

"You don't remember anymore?"

"No, only when I woke up in the hospital."

"That was really helpful. Thank you."

Emily smiled diffidently, looking relieved.

Loader addressed the room. "I think we are clear about the recollections of our patients, and nothing more can be gained at this time. I understand that they will be released tomorrow after final examination."

In the event, the patients were not released until the day after. All were given a clean bill of health.

The change in Emily was astonishing. Before the coma, she was a sweet-looking child, obviously suffering from physical and mental difficulties. Now, she was a beautiful young girl with a normal sparkle in her eyes and a skip in her step. She was excessively inquisitive, as if she had a lot to catch up on.

Tracey was over the moon, her face permanently radiating happiness. The trauma of having little money and frugal living mattered little to her; Emily was the only gift she'd ever wanted. Now that Susan had given her a permanent domestic position at the farm, and living accommodation, her cup was overflowing.

Claire continued to manage the farm observatory as an international visitor site. Susan continued to take an interest in the observatory and spent time preparing for her research project. All domestic duties were now carried out between the housekeeper and Tracey, leaving Susan free to concentrate on her project.

Loader was away most of the time. Susan didn't question his absences, reacting with pleasure when he did arrive at the farm, usually early evening. They both treasured their evenings together. Tracey turned out to be an excellent cook and would serve supper in the dining room. After which they relaxed in the living room, sitting together on the sofa, comfortable in their closeness.

Loader's love for Susan was well established; her own response was more reserved; Loader saw how her face lit up each time they met, but she seemed unsure to admit her own feelings.

He accepted that this was because of recent events; George's demise was still new, only six months ago. In addition, she had been comatose for ten days and believed she had been taken over by an alien! Not exactly a smooth path for love. Behind which was twenty years of marriage to an older man, where the relationship seemed driven by research, not love. Loader suspected that Susan had never experienced real love and probably didn't know how to love.

This evening, they sat as usual, together on the sofa, glasses of wine on the side table.

Something was different; Susan became aware of Loader's masculine presence, feeling a warmness invade her body, a feeling of curiosity and interest that confused her.

She detected a preoccupation in Loader's manner. He was clearly involved in something major but kept it to himself. Instead, he turned the conversation to Susan's own activities.

"So, Susie, tell me a bit more about the SGP project you're working on."

Loader's use of the diminutive 'Susie' unlocked something in her psyche. In twenty years of marriage to George, she had always been 'Susan'. 'Susie' was an intimate statement of a developing relationship, something that had been absent from her life.

This sort of intimacy she had never really experienced. Now, her closeness to Loader created responses that engulfed her. When they touched, she felt reaction that tingled deep within her.

She felt herself colouring and, to hide her confusion, responded in level tones. "Matt, it is so interesting. We are trying to formulate a programme for work and to divide the areas of study."

"Who is 'we'?"

"Oh! There are over one hundred scientists signed into the group. Matt, I only know a few. We have a small UK group based in Norwich. But a lot of the research programmes are in America and Germany."

"But the project?"

"It's something neuroscientists have been pondering for years," she said then, warming to the subject, added, "I'm sure you know that the brain is the most complex thing in the world, a whole level more complicated than, say, the most sophisticated computers."

"I give you that," he said, smiling, adding mischievously, "especially a woman's brain!"

Susan reacted with mock severity. "Matt! This is serious."

"Of course," he said contritely. "So, seriously, what is the project about?"

"Where to begin? We know a lot about the brain, Matt, how it works, how it influences every aspect of the body and human experiences. Great advances have been made in understanding its working. As I've told you before, this knowledge is helping to treat so-called incurable diseases and, recently, even paralysis. But there are a number of scientists who believe there is a missing link, and in our endeavours, we are missing that crucial link."

She paused, fervour in her eyes.

"Which is?"

"Well, I suppose you could say that we are looking for a link between the brain function and the soul."

Loader was growing more interested, mulling through the import of her words.

"The soul? That's pretty intangible, isn't it?"

"We are still on the edge of understanding the complexity of the brain, but there must be something else. The SGP call it the 'brain within the brain'. A sort of intelligence we have not even scoped."

"Hmm!" Loader eased his position and reached for his glass. "We're getting into the realms of philosophy here, Susie."

Susan laughed, and the spell of serious discussion was broken. She revelled in the diminutive use of her name, and they talked about generalities. She had forgotten the preoccupied mood that Loader had shown on his arrival, and he did not take it further.

Loader's phone rang. It was John in the observatory, his voice agitated.

"Matt, the signal's gone," he said, without preamble.

"Gone?" Loader tried to get his mind onto the sudden change of thought.

"Yes! Gone, there's no reception – something has packed up!"

"OK! We're coming." Loader dropped the phone, leaping to his feet. "Susie! The signal's failed. Come on!"

They hurried from the room and along the corridor to the observatory. There were several people in the room with John, all turning as Loader and Susan entered. The first thing Loader noticed was that the large monitors were silent, with just a line of white noise dancing along the screens. The room seemed suddenly empty. It was the first time Loader had ever seen the working monitors without the vibrant signal pattern and high-pitched noise, now just the soft background frying sound of the cosmic noise.

John held his arms open, a stunned look on his face. "It just stopped. Alec has checked the circuitry; everything seems to be OK. Just no signal."

"Right. What were you doing when it shut down?"

"Nothing really. These three gentlemen are visiting from the Southwest Astronomy club, I was just explaining how the signals were picked up and displayed when they just stopped." John sounded aggrieved.

"Has anyone been out in the antenna room?"

"No, why? Do you think the dish has been knocked off 'line of sight'?"

"I don't know, John. Alec, would you re-enter the coordinates and then check the receivers again?"

Alec nodded and went off into the antenna room.

Loader was trying to think what he could do. "What do you think, Susan?"

Before she could reply, Loader's mobile rang. It was Duncan from the SETI Institute.

"I've just been hauled out of goddamned bed, Matt! Our system seems to be down. What's going on?"

"No idea. We're down too. Alec is checking our alignment and circuits, but the fact you're down too indicates the transmissions have stopped."

Duncan said, "OK, we'll check it out with NASA. Keep us informed if you learn anything."

"Of course. Likewise, let me know what you find out." Loader rang off, turning to Susan.

"What now, Susie?"

Susan had become pale, looking around the observatory as if the answer was in sight. For years, the radio telescope had been a constant part of her life with George. The ethereal feel of electrostatics was gone, and the room felt empty and cold.

"I don't know, Matt; SETI Man has gone!"

Loader saw the loneliness that had returned to her eyes. All that she and George had lived with for over twenty years had just taken a step back.

Loader's heart ached to console her. "Not so, Susie," he said gently. "SETI Man was here; he visited you – look, the proof is Emily. You can't take that away."

"But why have they gone, Matt, why?"

"There has been circuit failure somewhere, Susie. Once Alec has found it, we'll be up and running again."

"*No*! I don't believe it, Matt. I believe that SETI Man came to look at earth because they detected intelligence here, then they've seen the appalling mess we've made of the planet and have left us to stew!" Misery showed in her face.

"Even so, if you're right, why come all this way, find intelligence here and then just ditch it?"

"I felt it, Matt, I felt it when I was dreaming, that whatever intelligence was with me wanted to plumb our 'depth' of intelligence. Having seen the state of the so-called 'intelligence' here, they have treated us as primitive and moved on."

"Come on, Susie, of course there is a lot of evil in the world, but there is good stuff too. Think of all the marvellous advances made in medicine and in pulling people out of poverty and so on."

Susan remained haunted.

"But these are just small pockets of success – weigh it against the evil that mankind inflicts on the world on a daily basis."

"Look," continued Loader, "look at Emily for example. We all love her; now look at the difference all this has made to her and to us."

Susan looked at Loader through troubled eyes. She saw his handsome face, wreathed in concern for her, felt a longing she couldn't explain. Suddenly, she wanted him close to her, holding her in his strong arms, and she felt comforted.

They returned to the living room, trying to talk about generalities, but conversation remained desultory, the events in the observatory weighing on their thoughts. In the end, they decided to call it a night. It was still early, but Loader had a lot on his mind.

"Susie, I shall be away for a while. I shall be leaving very early. Tomorrow. We'll stay in touch every day."

"What's a while?"

"A few days, hopefully not more. Anyway, it'll give you time to work on your project," he added, to lighten the mood.

They went upstairs together, pausing at Susan's door. She unlatched the door, standing uncertainly, an unfamiliar urgency consuming her body.

Loader leaned in to kiss her chastely goodnight, for a moment holding her close.

Susan momentarily responded, pressing against him, feeling his hardness against her. For a fleeting moment, she was lost, a deluge of emotion flooding through her.

Then Loader drew back. "Sleep well, my Susie," he said softly. "I'll be leaving very, very early; don't get up. I'll call you later in the day." With that, he gave her another gentle kiss and went to his bedroom.

CHAPTER 29

At 5am, Loader left the farmhouse and started the drive to Larkhill Barracks, which had become the operational nerve centre for Brown Bear.

He arrived at the main gate of the barracks at 8.50am. A meeting of the Brown Bear task force was scheduled for 9am. Loader entered the building five minutes late for the meeting, which was held up waiting for his arrival.

A throng of forty-two people were chatting in groups, coffee cups in hand, as he entered the room.

Bob Dixon came forward to greet him. "Morning, boss," he said, shaking Loader's hand. "We're all here now. Let's get you a coffee, then I'll introduce you."

Loader smiled at the roomful of faces turned to see him. He raised his hand. "Hello. Good to meet you all. Thank you for your time." After some shuffling, all were seated at the table, which comprised ten army folding tables pushed together. Loader and Dixon sat at the head of the arrangement.

Dixon took the chair. After a welcome, he invited the participants to introduce themselves.

First, on this right, was Loader's boss Nigel Phillips, followed by representatives of twenty-eight of the forty-three territorial police authorities, security forces, Special Operations groups and GCHQ.

"Thank you," said Dixon when the introductions were completed. "I will summarise the situation; then we will work out the way forward. Firstly, it is vital that we are on the same hymn sheet. I don't need to remind you that this operation is top secret, and just one loose word could at least compromise the operation, or at worst, set off a terrorist attack, the likes of which we have never seen. So, a very tight control of your men down to the bottom level.

"The mission: to target Turners Express Couriers. TEC. There are seventy vehicles employed by the company, mostly operating out of Basingstoke. We have determined that at least five vehicles are moving around the country with seemingly no agenda. At least twenty-five vehicles appear to be operating bona fide courier services to companies across the country but concentrated in areas of national security interest.

"We have allocated two OPS group per 'roving' vehicle. First OPS group, 'Bear 1'. Watch and report. Stick like the proverbial to a blanket. Do not apprehend. Do not be seen; report back daily. 'Bear 1' has been on the road for the past two weeks. We have a picture of which companies TEC deliver to, how often and where they pick up."

Dixon paused for questions. There were none.

"OK, the second group – 'Bear 2' – will be on twenty-four seven standby closely watching 'Bear 1'. This is a Special Ops group. This group will stay kitted up and ready to move on command and in coordination. There is a stick for each TEC site, made up of Special Ops military, Special Ops police, including bomb disposal."

A hand went up.

"A stick?" The questioner was a young-looking DCI.

Dixon grinned at him. "A stick is twelve active and armed personnel. There will be drivers and medics in the background." He went on. "Why are we doing this? Because, as of now, we regard TEC as a significant threat to our national security. And because the threat, TEC, has tentacles spread across the country, every move has to be closely coordinated."

Dixon paused. "Questions?"

The DCI, Yorkshire Constabulary, raised his hand. "So, what sort of goods do TEC transport?"

Dixon glanced at Loader. "Good question. TEC specialise in providing imported materials and products for white goods and garden equipment. The imported stuff is distributed to established companies, for finishing and assembly."

Another question: "What is it that we suspect TEC to be guilty of?"

Dixon grimaced. "Not fully clear. TEC is linked to a coded message from Moscow, which recently activated a covert Special Operations cell here in the UK, known as Brown Bear." He turned to Loader. "Do you want to add to this?"

Loader nodded. "Brown Bear is a Russian covert operation here in the UK. It worries us because Russia has been designated a rogue terrorist state for its incursions into Ukraine and senseless, indiscriminate bombing of civilian assets. This comes at a time when Russia has also increased its violation of international air and sea space over the past year.

"Our government is acutely aware of the threat that could face the UK and are ensuring that we are not caught with our pants down. The reason for this operation – Brown Bear – is that TEC have been directly implicated. Moreover, one of the five 'roving' TEC vans has been stopped. Extensive electronic surveillance equipment was found to be fitted into the back of the van. Forensics also found traces of explosives residue in the van."

"So, isn't TEC already alerted to our moves?"

"No, I hope not. The local police apprehended the driver in a contrived routine stop. They were instructed to accept the driver's excuse that the electronics were some sort of fancy sat nav equipment and let go. The driver did not know that forensics had found the explosives traces."

The meeting was still in full swing when the GCHQ representative Margaret Dibden's phone vibrated. She listened for a moment, then holding the phone up, and with an apologetic nod to Loader, left to the room. The meeting continued. Thirteen minutes later, she returned with Adrian Boyce. Loader recognised him from his previous visits to Cheltenham. Margaret Dibden looked serious. "Excuse me, Mr Chairman, Matt, you need to know this. Adrian has just driven down from Cheltenham with important updates; you need to factor this into your decisions today."

All faces studied the GCHQ newcomer.

Margaret went on. "Adrian Boyce is a senior analyst leading the work on the Brown Bear file."

"Of course," Loader responded. "Welcome, Adrian, the floor is yours."

Adrian Boyce came and stood at the head of the table. "Hello, everyone. As you have just been told, I am the senior analyst working on the Brown Bear files. My group has been receiving the data from the OPS-1 team for the past two weeks. Although it's not a primary task, we have been studying the data sent in from the field. What we did was to construct a set of scatter diagrams, one for each courier vehicle. Then, using Cartesian coordinates, we plotted the correlation between vehicle destination and frequencies." Adrian paused, his face serious.

"Our analysis, coupled with some conjecture, caused me to get down here ASAP to report to you."

"Go on," urged Loader.

"So, there are twenty-five scatter plots in the mix; each shows a similar result. Take one as an example. Van number seven, it operates in the Devon, Somerset and Gloucester areas. Over the past two weeks, we have plotted 240 deliveries. There is a fairly general frequency of deliveries to fifty destinations but a significantly higher number of deliveries to a specific business."

He paused as the meeting became suddenly more alert.

"This by itself is not significant. After all, one business could be using the courier exclusively for its business. But all twenty-five plots exhibited the same characteristic. We added another parameter." He spelt out his words with emphasis. "We added in the coordinates of major or strategic sites to the plots!"

The meeting waited, spellbound.

"Ladies and gentlemen, the businesses that received significantly more comings and goings are all within fifty miles of a strategic site."

Now there were murmurs and unrest in the audience.

Adrian went on. "Take our van number seven. It operates over a wide area from its depot in Basingstoke. Over the past two weeks, it has made an average of two or three drops to various companies in the area. For example, Taunton, Wellington, Shepton Mallet, Bath, Yeovil. But," he emphasised his words, "*fourteen drop-offs to Bridgewater* – one a day!

"So, we looked for some significance. The receiving company, Southwestern Tools, has a large facility on an industrial park just outside the town. Bridgewater is twelve miles from Hinkley Point nuclear power station!"

The delegates became restless, murmuring loudly.

Adrian raised his voice over the muttering. "We found that all twenty-five destinations were in a similar proximity to a strategic site, including five nuclear power plant sites and," he stressed the words, "*RAF Brize Norton, RAF Coningsby, HMNB Faslane* and so on."

Now everyone wanted to speak; there were questions; maps were put up on the screen as the possible impact of the data sunk in. Loader and Nigel Phillips conferred; Nigel placed an urgent call to the home secretary, calling for an urgent meeting of the Government.

He, Adrian and Loader set off for London. The remainder of the meeting delegates were to remain at Larkhill, continue planning and wait for further orders.

CHAPTER 30

Yet another COBRA meeting was hastily convened for 2pm.

All frontline cabinet members were present, as well as the chief of staff Sir Mark Forsyth.

The meeting was again chaired by the prime minister, Grace Armstrong. She wasted no time, calling on Loader to brief the meeting.

Faces became grim as the import of the GCHQ analysis became clear.

"We have to shut this outfit down!" Malcolm Bishop, Secretary for Defence, responded immediately.

"On what grounds?" demanded the home secretary. "What we've got is conjecture, maybe a big coincidence."

Other voices called for caution. "We could investigate one site and get to the bottom of it. There could be a quite plausible reason for the peaks in the graphs."

"Dangerous," replied Bishop. "If there is a terrorist plot here, examining one could set off the remaining sites before we get to them."

The meeting went on to discuss possible outcomes, including booby traps, legalities, collateral damage and, specifically, any international blowback.

Grace Armstrong listened intently to the debate. She made notes; she queried assumptions; she posed searching 'what ifs'. After two hours of debate, all bases had been covered.

She tapped the table for attention. "There are still many intangibles; we do not have any hard evidence of illegal activities, except the presence of explosives traces in one of the TEC vans. Is this enough to warrant a full-blown raid on twenty-five UK businesses? Conversely, we do have hard facts about the pedigree of the covert group Brown Bear from previous activities, including actual harm on UK soil. We also have the factual coded message from Moscow activating Brown Bear. On balance, I believe that the danger of doing nothing is outweighed by the need to protect our nation from even one outrage, even if only perceived.

"I therefore authorise the appropriate ministers and security agencies to take action to close down all the TEC sites immediately, using whatever means is necessary to protect themselves and wider damage. I expect this action to remain secret until activated."

The prime minister paused. There was an outbreak of table thumping as the more hawkish ministers applauded the decision.

She went on. "Right! Who is in overall command here, and are the assets in place to carry out the procedure?"

Bishop responded. "Yes, ma'am. All parties are in place. With your authority, we would plan coordinated zero at three-thirty on Friday morning."

"The day after tomorrow?"

"Yes, ma'am."

Loader called Susan, telling her he would be home that evening and would spend the next day with her at the farmhouse. It was a three-hour drive, so he expected to arrive about 8pm in time for dinner.

Susan put the phone down, realising an inner excitement. She visualised Loader, involved in some high-level business, his strong frame commanding attention, and she experienced an inner warmth. Years of abstinence were stripping away, replaced with a strange curiosity, triggering sensations in parts of her body.

When Loader arrived at the farmhouse, he was greeted with an unusually warm embrace.

Tracey had prepared the dinner for the evening. Loader greeted her with a friendly hug.

"Where's Emily?" he asked.

"Guess!"

"OK, I might have known! Please carry on and serve up; I'll just go and say a quick hello."

Walking through the corridor and into the observatory, Loader realised that the old buzz was missing. True, the cosmic noise still danced on the monitors, but there was no sense of proactivity. The observatory was empty, obviously no external visitors this evening. He continued into the antenna room; sure enough, Emily was seated on the sighting 'scope chair, a notebook on her lap and busy drawing.

Loader was pleased to see that she was using the picture book he had bought her.

Emily jumped from the chair, hurling herself into his arms.

"I knew you were coming," she said delightedly.

Loader held her close for a moment, feeling touched by her new persona. They chatted for a moment, Loader saying, "Well, Em, supper is about ready – are you coming along?"

They happily returned to the kitchen, hand in hand.

After dinner, Tracey and Emily returned to their own quarters. Susan and Loader sat in the living room, customary glass of wine in hand. They steered clear of heavy conversation, finding they could chat endlessly about trivial matters or exploring their earlier lives.

Soon, it was bedtime. Loader explained that he would stay at the farmhouse the next day but that a major event was taking place that night and he would have to leave around noon.

"More cloak and dagger stuff?" Susan asked lightly, trying to hide her disappointment.

Loader suddenly felt the pressures of the Brown Bear case and the awful consequences that would arise if things went wrong.

"Susie," he said, using her diminutive name, again evoking the tingle within her.

"I shouldn't tell you this; please treat it as very, very important and not a word."

She looked at Loader, her face tilted towards him with serious expression, her eyes wide, lips slightly parted. He began to feel he was sliding towards an abyss, longing to kiss her. Trying to pull himself together, he went on. "There is a big national security event tomorrow night. I'm afraid I must be there."

"Of course," she said with a slight edge.

"Once this is all over, I promise I'll take a break and we can take a holiday."

"OK," she said in a small voice.

"Right! I'll check the doors and lights, then it's off to bed."

Outside her bedroom door, she again paused uncertainly, her face uptilted for a goodnight kiss. The emotions she had experienced during the day returned, suffusing her body.

He leaned into her, his gentle kiss on her parted lips lingering, growing more urgent. He knew she felt his hardness, yet she, too, lingered.

"Susie," he whispered, "shall I come and sleep with you?"

For an answer, Susan edged the door open and, entering the room, left it open. Loader followed.

In the room, they both hesitated, then wordlessly, Susan gathered a nightgown that draped her pillow, disappearing into the bathroom.

Loader stood uncertainly. He had never been in the room before, looking around at the decor and soft furnishing, an elegance displaying evidence of Susan's hand. Modern furnishings blending seamlessly into the old-fashioned room. There was a dressing table against the wall at the foot of the bed with plenty of space between it and the bed. In one corner were two boudoir chairs and a small side table.

After a moment, he sat on the bed and took off his shoes. Was this the right side? In confusion, Loader, picking up his shoes, moved to the boudoir chair and sat down with his shoes at his feet.

Then he quietly got up and, opening the bedroom door, hurried to his own room. Bringing back his robe and toiletry bag, he closed the door softly behind him. He sat down again.

Susan emerged from the bathroom in her nightdress. Loader looked at her, his heart beginning to beat faster. She was a vision of loveliness, moving into the room. She seemed suddenly shy; head tilted gently, she said, "The bathroom's free."

Loader gave her a reassuring smile. "OK, won't be a mo."

He soon returned to the room in his robe; Susan was sitting at the dressing table, brushing her hair. She stood as Loader came beside her. She moved into his embrace.

"I love you, Susie," he said gently, kissing her forehead.

"I know," she said in a small voice, "I love you too."

She was in a loose embrace against him. He let his roble fall open, drawing her closer.

"You won't need this," he said, gently easing her nightgown from her shoulders, then enveloping her in his arms and drawing her against himself, wrapping his robe around them both.

The feel of Loader's warm, firm torso against her soft skin released a torrent of feelings in her body. Suddenly, her brain was taking charge of her emotions; she felt a tide of exultation ripple through her, and her body responded, alert and sensitive.

At the back of her mind, now ignored, was a curiosity, as if something unknown was about to take place.

Loader gently guided her to the bed.

CHAPTER 31

Four, three, two, one – go, go!

Precisely at 3.30am, in unison, across the country, twenty-five industrial units were quietly entered by shadowy figures, ominously black in the dark sky, armed.

Reconnaissance is everything! By the time the special operation was underway, non-intrusive surveillance had been conducted. For each group, the head of ops knew who was officially employed by the company, the layout of the premises, the use of night watch personnel, the record of CCTV cameras in the area, the main grid entry onto the site. All of which had been passed on to the commander of each group at pre-op briefings on the night of the operation.

Each of the twenty-five groups included, in support, senior members of MI5. Bob Dixon was accompanying Bear 10. Loader had briefed and allocated a senior agent to each team, electing himself to join Bear 4, the group allocated to raid an industrial site outside Bridgewater in Somerset. On the ground, the group commander was in control. He chose not to enter via the road entrance, which approached the front of the office block, choosing instead to direct his team to a vantage point about fifty metres to the side. The lead officer waited, bolt cutters ready. The team stood in file behind him, firearms held lightly across their chests. On the word 'go', the lead officer received a firm tap on the shoulder; a portal was quickly cut into the chain-link fence and the men silently jogged to the front of the offices. The lead man didn't bother to try the door; he had received information from intel about its construction. Two devices were Blu-tacked onto the door, a thick muffler propped over it. The team stood back along the wall to the side.

With a muffled explosion, the door gave way. Inside, the team knew which way to go; the leader, moving in a crouched jog, gestured and ran on. Two members peeled off, following the signals.

As they entered the shattered door, the power to the building failed. They continued by glow lamps. Loader followed behind, leaving one member back as a doorkeeper.

The team knew from intel that the company used a nightwatchman. They had to get to him whilst he was disoriented by the sounds and the power failure. They ran through the whole suite of offices, producing no result. The team went into the rear part of the building, which gave way to a large manufacturing workshop and roller door access to warehousing.

Loader hung back. It was not his operation. It was clear that the nightwatchman was not in the restroom as expected. Perhaps he was on an inspection of the premises.

The team cleared the workshops, raising roller shutters to reveal the warehouse area. The team fanned out to cover the cavernous building. Glimmer lamps would not do the job; the team switched to beam lighting. Suddenly, the area was illuminated by eight powerful LED heavy-duty lamps, revealing stark images of pallet shelving and dark shadows.

The team paused, uncertain where to start. The commander moved his torch beam slowly across the front of the shelving.

"Mother of God!" he whispered hoarsely.

Serried rows of shelving stretched into the depths of the warehouse. There, sitting on the shelves, were ranks of machines. It didn't take an engineer to see what they were.

Drones!

"There's effing hundreds of them!"

Loader still hung back in the offices area. He was making his way towards the warehouse when he caught sight of a movement in the shadows. Drawing his sidearm, he went to investigate.

Seeing a figure scurry across the corridor, Loader aimed his weapon, shouting a warning. The figure, running towards the exit, turned and, from a crouch, rolled an object along the passage towards Loader. Loader fired his weapon, seeing the man go down, then turned to run.

The corridor erupted in a blinding flash, the partition walls collapsing like cards. Loader was caught in the full force of the blast, hurled along the full length of the corridor and smashed against the end wall. Debris and partition walls fell over his prostrate body. Parts of the corridor fabric ignited in flames, quickly growing in intensity.

Amidst the din, voices were shouting, the raiding group rushing to the scene.

The commander roared in a controlled voice. "You, you, get into the workshop and look for fire extinguishers!"

At that moment, the officer left behind as rear doorkeeper called the commander on his mobile from the other side of the growing inferno.

"Loader's down, boss; I can't get to him," he shouted urgently.

"Stay where you are. Mark Loader and keep him in sight – we're coming round." Turning to the remaining team, he shouted, "Man down! Get round the front; find a way to get to him."

He called the police phalanx that was waiting a street away. "Man down! Get here, fast!"

With that, he ran into the workshop, looking for an exit to get him round the collapsed walls. He found a fire exit door, smashing it open; he ran back round to the front of the building and approached the growing inferno through the front offices.

The doorkeeper was there, peering through smoke and flames to a tangle of partition walling. He frantically pointed to the far corner; Loader's body could be seen lying face down, marginally protected by a fallen wall section. Debris continued to rain down over his cover.

Fire extinguishers had been located in the corner of the workshop. Three team members, all SAS veterans, turned the hydrant on themselves, until they were doused and sodden, then, racing to the collapsed corridor, thrust past the commander and doorkeeper, dropped to their knees and began crawling through the burning debris to reach Loader's body. Without ceremony, they grabbed his ankles and crawled backwards towards safety. Scorched and scarred, they collapsed into the main office, where they lay coughing and groaning.

Loader was unresponsive.

The approach road was suddenly filled with fire engines, police cars and two ambulances. The commander signalled to the hurriedly dismounting police and fire chiefs with his arm raised high, hand pointing down on his head, the universal signal known as 'come to me!'.

"I've got four casualties to be evacuated," he shouted in a controlled voice. "One unresponsive! Get them away, fast!"

The chief urgently signalled the paramedics forward. Rushing into the main offices, they kneeled over Loader, checking his vital signs, placed him into position for defibrillation but found he was breathing. Quickly and efficiently, they worked him over then, turning to the waiting bearers, shouted, "Get him away – he's alive."

Loader was hurriedly bundled onto a stretcher and into a waiting ambulance which tore off at speed. The paramedics turned their attention to the three rescuers, all three suffering from burns and cuts.

Seeing everything was being dealt with, the commander called the ops controller.

CHAPTER 32

"Hello, Susan, Bob here." Dixon's voice was restrained.

"Hello, Bob. Matt's not here; I thought he was with you?"

"It was you I wanted to talk to, Susan."

"Oh!" An icy finger raced down her spine.

Dixon went on. "Anyone with you, Susan?"

"No, just Tracey, in the kitchen. Is something wrong, Bob?"

"I'll explain everything. Susan, could you get Tracey please? Then I can tell you both."

"What? Why, Bob? Has something happened to Matt?" Her voice rose.

"Please, Susan, just get Tracey." Susan jumped to her feet and hurried to the kitchen.

"Tracey, please come into the living room – now!" Panicky, she returned to the living room.

"Tracey's here," she said anxiously.

Dixon's voice tried to calm her. "Please sit down with Tracey, OK?"

"Yes, yes. What's happened? Is Matt OK?"

"There was a security operation last night, Susan, you'll read about it in tomorrow's papers, I'm sure. Matt was involved. I'm afraid he's been hurt."

Icy fingers on Susan's spine became an icy fist, tightening around her.

"No!" she cried hoarsely. "What happened, is he OK? Bob, tell me!"

"Susan, Matt is alive but has been very badly hurt. There's no other way to say it. He's in a bad way."

Tracey couldn't hear Bob's side of the conversation, but Susan's anguish was obvious. She sat close to Susan, her arm around her back.

Bob went on. "He has been air lifted to Musgrove Park Hospital in Taunton for severe trauma care…"

Susan broke in, her voice frantic. "I want to see him, Bob. I can get there!"

"Whoa, steady, Susan! He is still in orthopaedic surgery and can't see anyone. I just want to tell you that we've arranged to fly you down here tomorrow morning. A helicopter will be at the farmhouse at nine o'clock. Please keep Tracey with you, Susan. She can come too."

Susan tried to compose herself. In a calmer voice, she asked, "What injuries has he got?"

"I don't know the details, Susan. The paramedics said he had numerous superficial injuries to his face and hands, but he has suffered severe trauma from the explosion, which hurled him against a wall. We will have a better picture in the morning. Anyway, you'll be here about ten o'clock. I'll be here to meet you. So sorry, Susan, he's getting the best treatment possible."

Susan's panic subsided, replaced with a cold fear.

"Alright, Bob, I'll be ready. See you tomorrow." She closed her phone, turning to be consoled by Tracey.

"Matt will be OK; you'll see. He's a very strong man."

The helicopter touched down on the forecourt island of Musgrove Park Hospital, Taunton, at 11am.

Bob Dixon was there to escort Susan and Tracey into the hospital. The helicopter departed; the road traffic released.

"I've spoken with Matt this morning," Dixon said, trying to reassure Susan. "He's longing to see you."

Susan's drawn face lightened a little. Loader was obviously awake and anticipating her visit.

Dixon went on. "He left ICU yesterday and has been moved into a trauma ward in the new wing."

As they passed the M&S coffee shop, Tracey said, "You go on in, Susan. I'm going to grab a coffee and catch up with you later."

After what seemed another long walk, they arrived at the ward. Dixon gave Susan a reassuring grip on her elbow as he knocked gently and opened the door.

"You go on in," he said. "I'll go back down and have a coffee with Tracey; we'll join you later."

Susan paused inside the door, then hurried to the bedside as she took in the dressings and plasters on Loader's face and head. His arm was heavily bandaged. She carefully leaned over him and kissed his cheek.

"Matt! What on earth have you been up to?" She tried to sound light-hearted. But her eyes welled, tears wetting her cheeks. She kept her face softly against his, but he noticed.

"Come on, Susie; it's OK – you can hug me. I won't break!"

The dam burst; she laughed and cried at the same time.

"Oh, Matt! I've been so worried."

"I know," he said simply. "Everything's OK now, my darling. I'll soon be back to normal." They chatted gently; Loader said little about the raids; the TV news overnight had already given wall-to-wall coverage of the events.

"I can't believe this has happened in our country."

Loader wanted to change the subject. He wanted to know how Susie's projects were progressing and what news there was about SETI Man.

"There's nothing!" she replied. "The world seems to have moved on, lost interest in the amazing events. The news now is about the terrorist plots and the growing global instability."

The conversation moved on to everyday matters.

"How is Tracey?" Loader asked.

"Ohh, she's here, Matt! She was frantic but so strong. She'll be along in a moment and Bob too."

"And Emms?"

"I don't think she knows anything, Matt. When she finds out about you, she'll go to pieces; you know how she worships the ground you walk on."

They were interrupted by the arrival of Tracey and Bob Dixon. Bob stood back as Tracey bent over Loader, sobbing.

Soon, everything returned to an even keel. Conversation became more light-hearted. They stayed for over an hour. Dixon could see that Loader was beginning to tire; he suggested they leave for a while and come back after lunch.

Susan was last to kiss Loader, her face gently against his for some moments.

Over lunch, Dixon received a call from the consultant treating Loader, suggesting that they meet in his office for an update.

"The good news is that Matt is recovering well from his wounds," the consultant started.

Susan immediately picked up on it. "Good news? That means there is also bad news?" she asked, her voice suddenly concerned.

"Well, it's early days yet," the consultant hedged. "He's making great strides, but he received quite a trauma to his spine. It may take some time to recover. At the moment, he has no feeling below his waist."

Dread filled Susan. "He didn't say anything about this," she said in a small voice.

"That's Loader!" Dixon said.

The consultant continued. "We're setting up a physio programme that will rebuild his lower back strength and repair the nervous system." He sounded reassuring.

It was decided that Susan would stay on at Musgrove for a while. Dixon booked her into the Castle Hotel for a week, while they learned more about Loader's aftercare.

Dixon was still deeply involved in the aftermath of the raids and had to return to London. He arranged a car to return Tracey to Norfolk.

Eight days passed before Loader was released from the hospital into home care. He was mentally exhausted, returning to the farmhouse with relief.

Just two days before, he had sat with Susan and the consultant to discuss his prognosis.

"I need to be frank," the consultant began ominously.

"We have concluded a week of tests. With physios, X-rays, CT and MRI scans for signs of brain damage. I've also used a myogram to check your spinal cord, with electro myogram tests for the electrical activities of the muscle/nerve group. We cannot detect any physical damage to the spinal structure. The myogram shows some disconnect in the nerve muscle path."

"So where does it leave me? What can I do to cure it?"

"There is nothing you can do, Mr Loader, except to keep to the physio programme that we have given you. It cannot cure you but will keep your muscles from wasting away."

"Will the nerves heal?" Loader asked bluntly.

The consultant looked at him directly. "There's never been evidence of paralysis recovering from this type of damage."

Susan gasped. "Will Matt always be like this?"

"I'm so sorry, Mrs Newby; there is no cure for this type of injury. I'm afraid Mr Loader will be confined to a wheelchair permanently."

There was silence as the implication sunk in. Loader's face was impassive; looking at Susan's stricken face, he felt a pressing, emotional avalanche of love for her. The life they had hoped for, longed for, could not play out. The anger and fear rose like bile in his throat. He violently swung the wheelchair around so that he faced away from the consultant and Susan.

His face, still covered with superficial scars, crumpled in despair. Tears welled in his eyes.

"Matt!" Susan jumped from her chair and stood behind him, clasping her arms tightly around his chest.

"Matt," she said again. "It's OK, my darling. We'll manage

– you'll see!" She laid her cheek against the top of his head, minutes passing as Loader regained his composure.

Oddly enough, his immediate thoughts were of far away, of days in Afghanistan as a young SAS officer, seeing many men injured, some blown to pieces. He remembered one specific young corporal sitting among the ruins of a building, the fog of war all around them. The paramedics had just finished treating him; his legs were missing, a helicopter racing to the scene to evacuate him. He looked up at Loader, grinning, his face blackened with explosives residue.

"We got here, boss!" the young soldier exclaimed jubilantly, oblivious to his injuries.

The cathartic image appeared vividly in Loader's mind. Tension drained from him, and peace suffused his body.

He reached his arms up to clasp Susan's arms, still around his shoulders.

"Yes, my darling, we'll manage," he said.

CHAPTER 33

Now back at the farmhouse, Loader and Susan began to pick up the pieces of shattered dreams. They made a few modifications to improve accessibility so that Loader was able to navigate the whole ground floor, including the observatory, in his wheelchair. The first floor remained an obstacle until the stair lift was installed. Loader kept a second wheelchair on the landing to transfer him from the stairlift.

Claire and John managed the business side of the observatory, which was becoming an educational and research venue, and still received regular visiting groups of astronomy enthusiasts. Tracey accepted the role of housekeeper, leaving Susan and Loader free to pursue their research.

Life began to take on a routine, everyone adjusting to accommodate Loader's circumstance. Emily had shown immediate and heightened empathy for Loader and, where possible, would sit close by him. Over the weeks, a strong bond formed between them.

Loader was technically working from home. He attended press room Zoom briefings as a *Daily Telegraph* correspondent. He received commission from the newspaper to cover relevant stories.

Susan became immersed in her search for the genesis of the psyche project (SGP) and she, too, worked mainly from home, using Zoom and direct contact with scientists from across the globe.

Loader received a call from Janet.

"Hi, Matt. How are things today?"

"Good, Jan. Every day is a new day, you?"

"Yes, good too. I miss you calling in so often." Her voice sounded genuinely sad.

"Yeah! But we talk longer!" he jibed. They both laughed.

"OK, Matt, Eddie has got a piece for you to put together. I'm sending you the reports and the link to a Zoom meeting."

"OK, Jan, subject?"

"Something about how the Russians are evading sanctions." They rang off, Janet's voice warm.

Passing the time, Loader wheelchaired to the observatory; it was so familiar a territory that he felt a comfort and warmth from being there. As always, the banks of circuitry were active, indicators blinking, but the electro static sense was absent from the room.

John was at one side of the large central desk, immersed in papers, prepared for the next seminar. Emily was there, too.

"I might have known you were here!" Loader exclaimed in mock chastisement. "Why aren't you at school?"

"Matt, it's Saturday!" Emily jumped up and rushed forward to hug Loader.

"So, what are you up to, interrupting John?"

John glanced up with a smile and a nod.

"I'm not interrupting, honestly. I'm learning about how radio astronomy works. It's awesome, Matt. Did you know that these pictures," she pointed to the large wall screen, "are a mixture of signals from a few years ago to zillions of years old?"

Loader grinned. "I guessed it was something like that. You going to be an astronomer then?"

"Yes, I am. John sometimes lets me speak to Mr Deacon and Jenny when they call."

"Well, you are a special person, Em, being the only young lady ever to actually meet someone from the stars!" His eyes caught hers, a sudden sparkling light causing her eyes to flash iridescently blue. She looked away. A fleeting moment, then it was gone. He joined John, spending some time reviewing the papers for the seminar. As they completed the task, he said, "Well, I'm off back to the kitchen, tea and cake, I think. You coming, Em?"

Emily jumped up, papers forgotten.

"Bye, John!" she cried as she barred Loader's exit.

"Oh! Alright then, jump on," he said in mock resignation. She sat on Loader's lap as he negotiated the corridors back to the kitchen.

After dinner in the evening, Loader and Susan relaxed in the living room in their now customary position. Loader, dismounted from the wheelchair onto the end of the two-seater sofa, Susan settling beside him. They exchanged notes of the day, subsiding into comfortable silence over a glass of wine.

Loader's hand rested on the front of his thigh; Susan covered his hand with hers, then rubbed her hand gently up and down his arm.

"Did you know that touch is the most basic and vital sense?" she asked conversationally.

"Well, I know I like touching you," he said mischievously.

"Matt, will you be serious!"

"Sorry." He looked contrite. "Go on."

She patted his hand, then gently ran her hand along his arms. "Our skin is the largest organ of the body, Matt, it is full of touch sensors, which makes it the most important way for the body to communicate with the brain."

Loader listened with a smile. He patted her hand on his arm.

"Well, I love your brain too," he teased.

"Stop it, Matt! I'm trying to be serious! This is a crucial area of our research. Touch is the single most important trigger for our brain and body harmony. Touch is crucial for building healthy relationships by stimulating pathways for oxytocin, serotonin and the neurotransmitter dopamine. It's an important element of our research. To touch someone you love is to acknowledge their presence and to communicate desire for them. It's profound – it heals, communicates, influences and soothes. Matt, are you listening?" she scolded.

"Yes, of course, darling. Please go on."

"Touch is fundamental to the human experience. Our body is a complex web of energy, Matt, powerful energy, that dissipates throughout all parts. As with electromagnetic energy, when it reaches an area with aerial-like tendencies, the hand and fingers, it can radiate in concentrated form. There are countless reports of the healing properties of hands and fingers, soothing, reassuring, healing. The touch between bodies connects directly to our vagus nervous system, carrying information between our brain and internal organs."

Susan's face was animated. Loader moved his arm around her waist and held her close.

"We will always touch," he said quietly, all too aware that the most fundamental touch was always to be denied to them.

His body ached.

They sat quietly, each wrapped in their own thoughts until, slowly, they returned to everyday topics, then listened to music for a while.

Susan suggested they should go to bed; it was a little early, but he accepted the process now took a lot longer and more effort. On the landing, Loader manoeuvred himself onto his upstairs wheelchair and they started along the corridor to his bedroom. Susan would help him get undressed and into bed and then carry on to her own room. Tonight was different.

"I think you should sleep with me tonight," Susan declared, pushing the wheelchair on past Loader's bedroom to her own.

"Susie, no! I… well, I'm not…" he cried incoherently, feeling unready to take this step.

"I know," she said. "Let us see how we get on."

In the bedroom, they went through the routine of getting Loader undressed and into the bathroom. Susan had gone back to Loader's room and collected his toothbrush and nightwear.

Even the short distance between the bathroom to the bed required the use of the wheelchair. Eventually, Loader was perched on the side of the bed, ready for Susan to swing his legs up.

"My pyjamas?" he asked.

"We'll manage without," she said, making it sound like no big deal, lifting his ankles up onto the bed, where he lay on his back.

Finishing her own preparations, she approached the bed; she was naked.

Loader's eyes took in her beauty, his desire coursing through his brain, his lower body unresponsive. An agony and embarrassment he could hardly bear.

Susan stood on his side of the bed, then, passing a leg over his body, she knelt astride him, her hands holding his waist.

"Susie," he said anxiously, "I don't know that I can…"

"My darling man. Let's just see how it goes." Her libido was heightened; leaning forward, she kissed his lips, savouring his taste.

She pushed one arm under his torso, feeling the spinal bones in the small of his back. She massaged them, judging from his responses where feeling stopped.

After a while, still holding his waist, she straightened her arms to lift herself slightly, her breasts pendulous, beautiful, erect nipples brushing Loader's chest.

"Touch me," she commanded. Loader complied, his longing intensifying with every move. He held the weight of her breasts in his hands, fingers teasing the excited nipples.

"Susie, I love you so much," he whispered hoarsely.

She lowered her wetness onto him, moving at first gently, a feeling of empowerment surging through her.

Loader sensed the fusing of their psyche and hugged Susan ardently, her face only inches from his own, her lips slightly parted, breathing strongly, her face flushed.

He looked into her eyes, which blazed iridescently blue, her gaze boring into his eyes, into his skull and into his soul. A climax of feeling crackled between them.

Loader couldn't unlock his gaze; he felt drawn into her very being. Suddenly, the compelling command from her flashing eyes exploded within him.

"SETI Man!" he cried hoarsely. "He's here; he did not leave us, Susan – he's here! Susie he's here with us!"

In a cry of climactic orgasm, his eyes rolled; he passed out, his arms relaxing back onto the bed.

Susan let out a loud moan, collapsing onto the bed by his side, heaving with exhaustion. Their breathing slowed as they drifted into the magic peace of fulfilment. They slept.

Susan did not know how long she slept, coming to slowly, her psyche still foggy. She stretched out her arm to touch Loader. He was not there!

She was abruptly fully awake, panicky, casting her eyes to the floor beside the bed, then across the room. Loader was standing in the bathroom doorway, holding onto the doorframe, looking across to her, smiling, with eyes that beamed pure love across the room.

"What time do you call this?" he quipped.

"Matt!" she cried, springing from the bed.

"*No!*" he commanded. "I'm coming back to the bed."

She subsided back onto the covers, wide-eyed. Loader straightened his back and, letting go of the doorframe, walked tentatively towards her.

"Go steady, Matt!" Susan implored.

Loader reached her, upright and unaided, and sat on the bed beside her. Astonished, Susan clasped him round his waist.

"I can't believe it. Matt, where? What's happened?"

Then they both chorused together, "SETI Man!"

The following days passed in a world of incredulity. And a reappraisal of their life. Of all the people least surprised by Loader's miraculous recovery was Emily.

"I just knew you would get better," she said simply but hugged Loader with more than usual enthusiasm.

Loader and Susan wandered about the house in an aura of mixed awe and nerves; it took days for the reality to really sink in.

The *Daily Telegraph* ran a short piece: '*Daily Telegraph* Correspondent Matthew Loader, who suffered a spinal injury while covering the raid by a terrorist cell in Somerset, has made a miraculous recovery'.

It did not take long for the media to link the recovery with the SETI story and to ask: 'Was the *Daily Telegraph* correspondent, Matt Loader's, recovery due to alien intervention?'.

The stories and conjectures raged for several days.

Loader and Susan were relaxing in the sitting room; it was late afternoon, with some heat still in the spring air. The doors were open onto the patio overlooking the paddock. The 'container city' had gone, and they were able to gaze across the field to the trees beyond.

Susan broke the companionable silence.

"I've been thinking."

"Uh oh!" Loader sighed, smiling at her.

"Well, what if…?" She paused, in thought.

"What if, what?" Loader encouraged.

"Well, my project group have been discussing how to proceed regarding the search for the link from our brain to our inner brain, our soul." She paused again.

"And?"

Susan turned her full gaze onto Loader. "What if SETI Man is a manifestation of the intelligence we are seeking?"

"Go on." Loader sat upright.

"Suppose the energy beamed to us is not 'green man' per se but energy from an alien source which is able to trigger our soul or inner brain."

"How trigger?"

"Well, say, boot up our inner, as yet unknown, part of the brain or programme the one we know about?"

"My God, Susie. That's a thought! Suppose you're right? It opens up a whole new approach for you."

"Us, Matt. If there is anything in this, it affects the whole of mankind."

"OK! Where do you go from here?"

"I need a meeting of the full SGP. We would need to start up a project to investigate. We would widen our remit to include the signals from space." Susan was getting enthusiastic.

"Except the signals have stopped."

"Yes, well." Susan looked crestfallen.

"Susie, you know when you and I… well, when I recovered."

"Of course, Matt."

"The radio telescope signals had stopped well before then, but you cured me. Say SETI Man was inducted into you permanently?" Susan looked wide-eyed.

"Say you're right, and me and Emily and the others are SETI Men."

They chuckled; both had risen from their seats and were pacing back and forth. Loader's military training took over.

"Right. You want a project? And perhaps we need to include the observatory into the mix. I can take care of the radio telescope side, while you get your scientists on board and come up with a research plan for the overall project. Eh?"

"So, let's get to it tomorrow morning, Susie. Meanwhile, I see that the sun is over the yardarm."

Nigel Phillips welcomed Loader back.

"So pleased for you," he said. "It's good to have you back. Bob Dixon has picked up your job, but how do you feel about something new that's beginning to test everyone's minds?"

Loader was enthusiastic. "Yes, it will be good to get back to normal, Nigel. I really appreciate your support, but can you give me about a month? I've got a few things to sort out, like a wedding for example!"

Phillips laughed. "Of course. Congratulations, Matt. Well done. A month is fine. You'll be working with Bob Starkey; you might know him – he's MI6, their mid-east desk. I'll forward some files to your secure address for you to get up to speed."

"That's great. I'll get my feet wet ASAP – what's the project?"

"We've had some disturbing snippets from Starkey. We believe there is contagion from the Ukraine business. I want to open a new desk to cover it. I don't believe that we've seen the end of the story yet."

CHAPTER 34

Cyprus, the island of Aphrodite, the goddess of love.

Loader and Susan alighted from the plane at Paphos in twenty-nine degree heat; a warm breeze caressed them as they walked to the terminal building. Susan looked so carefree in a simple sundress and sandals, her hair tied back. A taxi took them to the Elysium Hotel along roads lined with a riot of orleander and hibiscus. Walls on route were covered in profusions of red and pink bougainvillea. Suddenly, the stresses of the past year just soaked away.

They had just one short week! The first day, they lingered over buffet breakfast and then wandered around the hotel and grounds down to the seashore where a small hotel beach and swimming area had been created. They spent the morning on loungers, at peace, soaking in the sun. They applied sunblock on each other, relaxing and chatting endlessly. After a light lunch, they tried different loungers at the poolside. In the early evening, they showered, changed, then strolled onto the main road for a while, finding a Chinese restaurant. They sat contentedly, drinking brandy sour, deciding what to eat.

On their return to the hotel, they came across a party in full swing on the outside patios. A local band was leading exuberant dancers in versions of *Zorba the Greek*. The dancers, mostly international tourists, pranced happily in confusion to the dramatic chords of the guitars.

Loader looked at Susan. "Shall we?" He grinned.

Susan at first demurred but then gave in to the hypnotic mood of the party, and they joined the revellers, trying to decode the intricate steps and the increasing tempo of the music.

Everything about each other was a new and exciting experience. They were learning what they liked, what they felt, what pleased them, what made them angry; there was a whole lifetime to explore their innermost feelings.

The next day, they hired a car and drove northwards to Polis and Latchi. These little towns consisted of no more than a street of restaurants and some souvenir shops, but it was relaxing, and the warm air continued to blow over them. They drove to the Anassa Hotel and sat on a wide terrace for lunch, looking down over the beach and coastline. There were few people around, and they sat in almost solitary peace. Lunch consisted of a village salad, feta cheese, olives and bread.

They lingered, finding that they could talk for hours about anything and everything. Loader could not get enough of knowing about Susan, and she wanted to know all about his work and his early life.

They visited tourist areas: Limassol, the promenade, along the coast, the souvenir shops. They drove to Pissouri and sat in the taverna on the beach, just whiling away the magical moments in a haze of peaceful contentment. On the fourth day, they drove to the Troodos Mountains and enjoyed a different view of Cyprus: greener, cooler and serene. Everywhere they visited were the typically Greek Cypriot taverns. They lived on village salads, kleftiko – Cypriot lamb – and fresh fruit. Wherever they went, the locals took to Susan; she responded to their warm friendliness, Loader watching the tiredness of years of sacrifice to the single project ebbing away.

There was a sense of timelessness about the island that captivated them; they wished they had more time, but the week passed all too quickly.

As they flew back to England, they vowed they would return.